C000273246

Even Cowgir

My Own Private Idaho

Even Cowgirls Get the Blues
My Own Private Idaho

Gus Van Sant

faber and faber
LONDON · BOSTON

Stills for *My Own Private Idaho* and *Even Cowgirls Get the Blues*
© Abigayle Tarsches
Portraits of Gus Van Sant and stills from *Mala Noche* © Eric Alan Edwards
Stills of *Drugstore Cowboy* and *Chimes at Midnight* courtesy of BFI Stills, Posters and Designs

Special thanks to Judith Verno and her associates at New Line Cinema

CIP records for this book are available from the British Library
and the Library of Congress

ISBN 0 571 16920 1

Printed in the United States of America

Contents

Gus Van Sant: Swimming Against the Current

The following interview with Gus Van Sant mostly took place at his rented apartment near Castro Street in San Francisco in April 1993. Van Sant had located himself there in order to begin pre-production on *The Mayor of Castro Street*, a film adaptation of Randy Shilts's biography of Harvey Milk, the city supervisor whose 1978 assassination (alongside that of Mayor George Moscone) made him a martyr for gay rights. Shortly after we talked, Van Sant quietly withdrew from the project, unwilling to direct the version of the script that Oliver Stone and his fellow producers wished to make. It is indicative of Van Sant's independent spirit that he should opt out of a movie that would have featured a bigger star (Robin Williams had been mooted as Harvey Milk), demanded a much bigger investment and got a wider distribution (from Warner Bros.) than each of his previous films. It was a decision that echoed Van Sant's taking *My Own Private Idaho* from a major studio, TriStar, to an aggressive indie, New Line, at a time when the integrity of that particularly personal film had also been compromised. But if this singular director has elected at times to drop down (or off) the big-budget scale to protect his interests, on a purely artistic level he has, in less than a decade, moved from minor to major.

Van Sant's emergence coincided with the lionizing of American independent film in the mid-eighties, an event spurred by the liberal arts media's dissatisfaction with commercial movies and the critical successes of directors like Spike Lee and Jim Jarmusch, specifically the latter, whose *Stranger Than Paradise*, winner of the Camera d'Or at Cannes in 1984, set a style for hipster road movies that has been the genre-of-choice for indie filmmakers since. At Cannes two years later, Jarmusch's *Down by Law*, Lee's *She's Gotta Have It*, and Lizzie Borden's *Working Girls* aggrandized the notion of a cohesive American new wave that has latterly been augmented by the arrival of Hal Hartley, Nancy Savoca, Steven Soderbergh, Todd Haynes, Richard Linklater, Allison Anders, Quentin Tarantino, Sadie Benning, and others. In fact, it is, by its very nature, a disparate movement with no single unifying methodology beyond the guerrilla warfare for backing, a non-studio visual aesthetic, and minority or existential themes (hence the preponderance of road movies).

The director of *Mala Noche* (1985), *Drugstore Cowboy* (1989), *My Own Private Idaho* (1991), and *Even Cowgirls Get the Blues* (1993) stands both inside this loose circle of filmmakers and on its perimeter. Based in Portland, Oregon, and therefore distanced from Hollywood and the indie ferment of New York, Van Sant has certainly inhabited the road genre, but he has extended it to a detached, serio-comic celebration – if 'celebration' can admit so much irony – of outsiderdom and alienation that is nonetheless more emotionally wrenching than, say, Jarmusch's deadpan, synchronous beat fantasies or Hartley's droll, deliberate meditations on young lovers thwarted by happenstance and meddlesome parents. Van Sant's heroes are invariably obsessives and seekers doomed to fail (though as critic Donald Lyons has pointed out, in losing they 'somehow win'*). They are gay men stoically suffering the torments of unrequited love, junkies, male hustlers, and, in *Cowgirls*, a woman hitch-hiker – they are riff-raff, society's detritus, who are ennobled not by any indulgent affection for lowlife on behalf of Van Sant, but by the simple fact that he refuses to moralize about them, to condemn or condone them. What Van Sant actually does do is demythologize their rebel status by making us spend quality quotidian time with them; thus in *Drugstore*, the carrot-topped dealer played by Max Perlich talks TV trivia as much as he does drugs; Matt Dillon's narrator/protagonist Bob may be the swashbuckling leader of his gang of drug-raiders, but he's also a boyish golfer with a clumsy backswing. Van Sant makes these outlaws ordinary.

Attempts to deify the director himself as any kind of

---

*'Gus Van Sant', *Film Comment*, September–October 1991, pp. 6–12.

counter-cultural hero come unstuck, despite his hip attributes. (Van Sant, who hopes one day to film Michael Murphy's *Golf in the Kingdom*, is, like Bob, a keen golfer struggling to get his handicap down.) Palpably influenced by William S. Burroughs (*Drugstore*'s proselytizing junkie priest), John Rechy (*City of Night*), Andy Warhol (whose voyeuristic imperatives and laconic detachment he shares), and Antony Balch (who filmed Burroughs shooting up in *Towers Open Fire*), Van Sant is at the vanguard of so-called 'queer' cinema in America. But that's more because directors like Haynes, Benning, and Tom Kalin have yet to achieve his commercial and critical success than because of the polemical vigour of Van Sant's work. Although the Harvey Milk film would have inevitably been activist, Van Sant is essentially a gay director of films rather than a director of gay films (*Drugstore*'s two couples are straight; Cissy Hankshaw's lesbian adventures in *Cowgirls* are not overtly political). In allowing himself to filter the stories he chooses to film through his own taciturn, egalitarian, and wry sensibility rather than being led by a predetermined agenda, Van Sant makes the gay (or junkie, or hitch-hiker) experience more readily communicable to wide audiences than the more self-consciously homoerotic or strident films of some of his contemporaries. Sexual orientation is less of an issue in his work than common emotions like repressed desire or the ache for family and home. Sex itself in Van Sant's films is Warholian: cold, commercial, elliptically framed.

Van Sant has spiralled from the neo-noir expressionism of *Mala Noche* to a loose, jagged, naturalistic style that has incorporated time-lapse photography, home movies, modernized Shakespeare, surrealism (the drug hallucinations in *Drugstore*; the Magritte-like 'face' at the end of the blacktop in *Idaho*), jokey tableaux (*Idaho*'s living, breathing porno magazine display), and ubiquitous playfulness. I make a claim for him as one of the great visual poets of modern cinema, an inheritor of Welles's theatricalism and Pasolini's low-life lyricism — less classical than romantic, though steeped in avant-garde experimentalism. Far more a laureate of the Pacific Northwest than the David Lynch of *Twin Peaks*, Van Sant anticipated the power of insalubriousness as a style before grunge became the region's high-export contribution to nineties rock culture.

He was born in Louisville, Kentucky, in 1952, the son of middle-class parents, Betty and Gus Van Sant Sr., a travelling salesman who became a sportswear and women's clothing company executive. The family moved to Darien, Connecticut, and then to Portland, where Van Sant attended the progressive Catlin Gabel School before enrolling as a film major at the Rhode Island School of Design. In 1976, after spending some time in Europe, he moved to Los Angeles, joining the Paramount-based staff of writer/director Ken Shapiro, who had spun a cult movie from hit TV show *The Groove Tube*. Having directed a short, *The Discipline of DE*, which was shown at the New York Film Festival, Van Sant was encouraged by Shapiro to circumvent the Hollywood machinery and raise independent money for his own projects, and in 1981, supported by his father, he directed his first feature, *Alice in Hollywood*. A screwball comedy about a would-be Hollywood starlet who does time on Sunset Boulevard before she makes it on TV, it was neither completed nor released and, disappointed, Van Sant returned to the East Coast. He worked in a warehouse and then with a Manhattan ad agency, writing scripts in his spare time. The money he saved enabled him to finance *Mala Noche*, based on a novella by Walt Curtis, an underground poet in Portland, which Van Sant turned into his own city of night, shooting the movie in shimmering black and white, replete with looming close-ups and haunting expressionistic angles. With the pathetic-comic saga of Walt (Tim Streeter), a convenience store manager who's forlornly in love with a Mexican teenager, the movie set a tone of cool despair and implied sado-masochism: like Bob in *Drugstore* and Mike (River Phoenix), the narcoleptic street boy in *Idaho*, Walt is anguished beneath his sexy, insouciant demeanour; like Bob and Mike, he loves someone who is destined to leave him; like them, he is last seen travelling to a new adventure or some kind of oblivion. Sissy Hankshaw, the pregnant 'progenitor of a tribe' at the end of *Cowgirls*, is the first Van Sant protagonist to find serenity and promise continuity.

Van Sant is still to make a studio film–*Drugstore* was produced by the now defunct Avenue Pictures and *Idaho* and *Cowgirls* by New Line–although he is likely to direct Buck Henry's screen adaptation of *To Die For* for Columbia as his next project. He himself has assured continuity as an American *auteur* if he can preserve his own corner of the field, his own private Idaho, although serenity is unlikely to become one of the watchwords of his oeuvre–we look to him to unnerve us more than we do to comfort us. That unsettling process, however, is never gratuitous or cheap (nor yet Lynchian). If Van Sant corroborates our sense that life *is* unsettling, marked by yearnings rather than by the cosy affirmations that Hollywood habitually offers, his resilient humour protects both us and his protagonists from maudlin responses. Melodic in their realism, unflinching in their acceptance of death, and anti-sentimental, Van Sant's films are as sure, as adult, and as commanding as those of Howard Hawks–*Drugstore Cowboy* as jaunty in its eulogizing of professionalism as *Only Angels Have Wings, Even Cowgirls Get the Blues* a perverse feminist analogue to *Red River*. There is, of course, no higher accolade.

Graham Fuller
June 1993

GRAHAM FULLER: *What are your earliest memories of needing to express yourself in an artistic way, through painting or writing?*

GUS VAN SANT: When I was about twelve or thirteen, I had this teacher—Bob Levine, his name was—in junior high school, and there was a whole group of students who religiously took his art class. We all *had* to take the class, but a bunch of us worked after school because we were entertained by him and he encouraged people. He, I think, was my inspiration in the early days. I actually remember him creating paintings in class, and then, on my own, I would emulate his style of painting, which was sort of the New York advertising world illustration style, design- or magazine-oriented as opposed to fine art. There was another, famous Robert Levine who did illustrations—I remember him doing one for Aqueduct Raceway—whose style was actually quite a bit like my teacher Robert Levine's style. It was the kind of stuff that was similar to what Warhol did in the fifties, except that it was in the sixties. I remember it being acrylic mixed in with tissue paper and then paint and gold leaf. I think of it as this kind of Greenwich Village, gay thing, because my teacher was an out gay teacher in 1963, which was pretty unusual for this very WASPy area where I lived in Darien, Connecticut. So, he was an early influence. Also we were doing a lot of silkscreening, just as Warhol was at that time, unbeknownst to me because I didn't know who Warhol was. We silkscreened posters and occasionally we would do artistic, multilayered silkscreens that were more like works of art.

Then there was our English teacher, David Sohn, who encouraged us to make films. He was a progressive writing teacher who had written this book called *Stop, Look and Write*. It was a book of photographs, and the point was to look at a photograph and then write about what might be happening in it. It was kind of McLuhan-esque, and I think David even recommended McLuhan in his class—pretty unusual reading for fourteen-year-olds. He also showed us *Citizen Kane* and Canadian Film

Board films that were definitely influenced by McLuhan, because they were an abstract barrage of voices and media images that didn't necessarily make sense. I remember writing a visual piece in David's class—like an illustrated novel, but short, ten pages or so. I still have that.

GF: *You also made some animated shorts with your parents' home-movie camera.*

GVS: We'd emulate guys like Norman McClaren and Robert Breer in our spare time and then show the films in class; although I don't remember ever showing a film myself. We'd come to Robert Levine and explain things that we'd seen over in David's class and I remember the art teacher being jealous of the English teacher. He claimed that they were art films and they weren't appropriate for the English class! Anyway, between the two of them, I was influenced a lot.

GF: *Do those teachers know your films?*

GVS: Oh, I'm sure. Bob Levine came to the opening of *My Own Private Idaho* at the New York Film Festival.

GF: *At what stage did you make* The Happy Organ?

GVS: During one summer I worked in my dad's company's mailroom on Fifth Avenue in New York and I spent the money that I made on a really developed Super-8 camera. I made films with that for a couple of years and then we moved to Oregon. Eric Edwards and I, who were friends in high school, decided to make *The Happy Organ* for our senior project; Eric later shot *My Own Private Idaho* and *Even Cowgirls Get the Blues* with John Campbell. Originally, the school project was just going to be in 8mm, but we decided to make it in 16 with sound. It was about twenty minutes long, black and white.

GF: *It was about a brother and sister who go on a weekend trip and the sister gets killed on the road. Where did that come from?*

GVS: I don't know. I just made it up. Fiction.

GF: *After that, in 1970, you went to the Rhode Island School of Design but you more or less gave up painting there. Why was that?*

GVS: Well, I painted at RISD, but I majored in film. Most of the kids there were painters or photographers or architects. Most people were interested in film, and maybe some of them went into filmmaking like I did, but nobody that I knew went to the school specifically for film, because the department was pretty small; it was known as an art school, though there were jewellery-makers and fashion students there, too. I remember a lot of students were very eager to get out of painting because there was apparently no future in it. Not too many students who had graduated with painting degrees had really gotten anywhere with their paintings.

GF: *David Byrne was there at that time, wasn't he?*

GVS: And the rest of the Talking Heads. Chris Frantz was taking one of the video courses and I remember he got his friends – David was one of them – to mime 'Mustang Sally' to a record, and they pretended they were a rock band on video. That was the first thing that I ever saw the Talking Heads do. I don't know if it was a statement, but it was like a funky art video. They wore wigs and fooled around.

GF: *Was there something in the air at RISD at the time?*

GVS: Yeah, the Providence Aesthetic, as Mary Clark used to call it. Mary Clark was a member of the Motels, which came out of sixties rock 'n' roll and drug influences. There was a bunch of art bands that were influenced by Martin Mull, who was a painter at RISD in the sixties and had a band called Soup. He was kind of the grandfather of my generation, though I didn't know him. A guy named Tim Duffy had a band called Snake and the Snatch and there were other bands like Iron Grandmother and Electric Driveway; they all had the same lineup, but they would change their costumes and come out and play as different bands from different eras. They were comedy-oriented, multimedia bands – 'painter bands' I would call them because none of the people in them were musicians, although they put together these shows which had very funny lyrics and a lot of pageantry and costume changes. Some people did performance pieces on stage, like one girl sat under a sun lamp for fifteen minutes between sets. Frank Zappa and the Mothers of Invention were probably an inspiration for all these people and I think everybody was influenced by the Velvet Underground at the time – because they were a painter band – and by the Warhol scene.

Nearly everybody stayed in Providence and most of them still live there and work as bartenders or teachers or whatever. But the Talking Heads – David, Chris, and Tina [Weymouth] – went to New York and forced themselves to stay there and pursued *serious* music as opposed to the Providence Style, which was not serious!

Meanwhile, I had left for LA. But that whole scene had had a real strong effect on me. There were two guys, Charlie Clavery and Scott Sorensen, who had a video project called *Meet the Stars*. If someone famous came to town, they would try to get in the backstage door without credentials, and see how far they could get – and that was the video! Charlie would act like a newscaster, except he'd wear a wig or funny glasses, and he would try and get an unauthorized interview and sometimes he would succeed. To this day I'm influenced by them and by the Motels and the multimedia approach and the humour within their projects. You don't really see a direct kind of influence in my work; it's just that they were inspirational. Some day I'd like to make a film about them.

GF: *What films were you seeing at this time?*

GVS: I was mostly influenced by the sixties experimental filmmakers who were also painters, like Stan Brakhage, Warhol, Ron Rice, Taylor Mead, Jordan Belson, who is a San Francisco painter; a lot of the San Francisco Canyon Cinema co-op people and the New York Anthology Film Archives people like Jonas Mekas. I don't think that I was directly influenced by anyone else, except to try and emulate commercial filmmakers and assimilate drama into my films once I had left RISD. The very last film I made there, my senior project, had an experimental tack, but it tried to incorporate a slick Hollywood format, like the Godard films. Although I didn't know much about Godard, and I still don't, I've realized that that was something he was doing. His films tended to look like

Hollywood films, but their stories and techniques were messed with and mixed up. I did something like that in a film called *Late Morning Start*. It was a failure, really, but it looked good and it was interesting. Its intention was to draw you into all these different stories, but not show you what happened; your attention was continually diverted. Bunuel's *Le Fantôme de la Liberté* did exactly the same thing, but I did it less successfully because I didn't have the budget.

GF: *When you moved to Los Angeles in 1976, you worked for a couple of years as a production assistant for writer-director Ken Shapiro. Tell me about that experience.*

GVS: Shapiro was working at Paramount. He had started *Channel One*, which was really the origins of *Saturday Night Live*-type skit humour. It was like hippie performance theatre and *The Village Voice* dubbed it *The Groove Tube*. They were also working with video and made a lot of fake commercials for things like drugs.

Ken took *The Groove Tube* on the college circuit and realized that there was a big market for this kind of thing. So he used his own money that he had saved up from being a child star in the fifties—he had appeared on *The Milton Berle Show*—and recreated *The Groove Tube* on 35mm film. It was a pretty slick production. The reason I started working for him was that Chevy Chase had done this interview in a *Los Angeles Times* Sunday supplement, and he said he was going to visit his old friend, Ken Shapiro—this was around February '76. So I looked Ken up in the phone book and called him, and he put me to work as his assistant because all his friends had left to do *Saturday Night Live*. At the time, Lorne Michaels was working for Ken as a writer, and they were writing this thing called *Ma Bell*, which was about Joey Schneider's rip-off of the phone company—an 18-year-old guy tampering with the phone system. It was about Phone Phreaks and it was a pretty exciting project. Ken was a very counter-cultural sort of person who smoked joints during the day as he wrote, scheming on his next film project for Paramount. At the time, it seemed like the kids were taking over the studios. As Ken's assistant, I thought it was going to be Easy Street for me from then on, which wasn't true. He did make a film called *Modern Problems*, but he became very negative about the studio system.

GF: *Why didn't you stay in Hollywood?*

GVS: I was being paid by Paramount through Ken, and when his contract ran out, he didn't hire me any longer. During the shooting of *Modern Problems*, I was the odd man out, because his wife got the job as his assistant, and there were too many producers involved for him to get all his friends jobs. So I didn't get to work on that one.

GF: *Around that time you directed a film called* Alice in Hollywood. *What became of it?*

GVS: It exists. I never sold it. I should probably try and sell it now.

GF: *You could probably find an audience for it now.*

GVS: Maybe. At the time I couldn't. When I finished it, I tried entering it into the LA Film Festival and the Atlanta Film Festival, but they wouldn't take it. So I felt like it didn't have a market at all. It was supposed to be a feature-length film, and I didn't think it really held up at an hour and a half, so I cut it down to forty-five minutes. It was a kind of ridiculous comedy, which is a dangerous area to work in. Even the big-budget films that attempt the ridiculous comedy genre fail. I was trying something too difficult, although I didn't know it at the time. I never got my money back from that.

GF: *Did it have any of the ideas that you've explored since?*

GVS: Yeah, some of them are quite similar because I wrote the script. But other little films that I made had a more serious edge; it didn't have that.

GF: *It's about a girl who comes to Hollywood and ends up living on the street, right?*

GVS: She ends up living in a car and eventually achieves notoriety as a television actress. Then she leaves her street friends behind because she's found a different strata of people. I think it was a comment on Hollywood friendships; the way I guess I'd learned to know them.

How people climb up a certain ladder and have business relationships instead of personal ones. It had that side to it, but it wasn't really stressed. The other side was this absurd comedy that was supposed to be a take-off of *Alice in Wonderland.*

GF: *You wrote several scripts around this time, including* The Corporate Vampire *and* Mister Popular. *What can you tell me about those?*

GVS: They exist as scripts. I wrote *Corporate Vampire* in New York. It was about a corporation that had a very exclusive higher echelon of presidents and vice presidents that were all vampires and a man who is promoted and initiated into their group. It's a *Rosemary's Baby* kind of thing. *Mister Popular,* originally called *The Projectionist,* was a story about a high school kid who influences his fellow students by subliminally introducing advertising images through audio-visual techniques. He gets the student body under his control and becomes the most popular kid in the school. I wrote it while I was living in Hollywood as the next project that I was going to do after *Alice.*

GF: *When you came to live in New York in 1983 you worked in an ad agency. Did you direct commercials?*

GVS: No, I was a junior producer. I did the technical work of booking mixing stages, that sort of thing. It wasn't really that important, what I was doing. I organized the company's slide show and stuff like that.

GF: *But you were able to save up enough money to make* Mala Noche.

GVS: Right.

GF: *What was it about Walt Curtis's novel that appealed to you? Why did you want to turn it into a film?*

GVS: In 1977 I had gone up to Portland to work on this film, *Property,* directed by Penny Allen, who had gotten a CETA grant for about $80,000. I was the sound man and Eric Edwards was the cinematographer. One of the lead actors was Walt Curtis, who was a Portland poet. He had, along with Mississippi Mud, a non-profit organization, printed this book called *Mala Noche.* And I remembered it as being really strong. It was Walt's first semi-novel; it was like a journal, in a way, one of the few prose things that he had written. I was writing a few things at the time but I thought *Mala Noche* was better than anything I was writing, and I knew that Walt would probably let me film his novella. Also, I could go back to Portland, which is where I wanted to live. There was a small film community there with one or two cameras floating around and some aspiring filmmakers who I could probably get to help me out. So I moved there to make the movie.

I thought *Mala Noche* was the kind of story that Hollywood wouldn't ever make and it was my new philosophy that my next project *should* be something they wouldn't ever make. That way you could keep it pure, simply in terms of the subject matter.

GF: *Were you consciously setting out to tell a story of unrequited gay love, or was it just unrequited love?*

GVS: No, it was unrequited gay love for sure. But I thought that if it was a good movie, it would relate to anybody – not solely to a gay audience. I had seen some gay films in Hollywood before I had left and had been to a gay film festival in New York. I witnessed how basic the films were at those festivals, and how there was a large audience that came to see them but there wasn't really any product, not even in low-budget films. *Taxi Zum Klo* came out before I made *Mala Noche*, and I think it was really the first independent film about gay life that did well in the regular marketplace. It became quite a big hit in certain cities around the United States, even in Portland, attracting straight as well as gay audiences. I remember that being a cue that I could maybe film Walt's story and get my money back. When you're making a film you always wonder whether or not it will break even.

GF: Mala Noche *coincided with* My Beautiful Laundrette *in 1985. Both films were significant in the way that they presented love between men without turning it into a polemical issue or a forbidden fruit.*

GVS: *Mala Noche* didn't really get shown that year, but it was at the Berlin Film Festival at the same time. I remember there was this Australian guy who I hoped would buy

Mala Noche, but he spent all his money on *My Beautiful Laundrette. Mala Noche* played at gay festivals for a few years, but nothing really happened to it until *Drugstore Cowboy* came out. It finally broke even this year. It only cost $25,000 and it's taken almost ten years to make its money back.

GF: *At times the cinematography of* Mala Noche *reminds me of* Touch of Evil. *You used a lot of huge close-ups in it, a very tightly packed frame, and some very weird expressionistic angles. How did you arrive at that style?*

GVS: It was probably a combination of things. It was black and white and Orson Welles's cinematography and David Lynch's *Eraserhead* were very influential. David Lynch had a certain lighting style – pretty minimal, but also very expressionistic – which I adopted when we were lighting interiors. He used spotlights and so I got a bunch of spotlights. Stanley Kubrick's black and white films were another influence.

GF: *The sequence in* Mala Noche *where you first see the home movie is surprising because it's in colour. You used home movies again in* Drugstore Cowboy *and* My Own Private Idaho.

GVS: *Paris, Texas* used home movies and I think I had seen it just before I began *Mala Noche.* There was a passage in *Mala Noche,* the novel, where the boys take photographs, but I had them making movies instead; it worked much better.

GF: *Pepper, in that macho Chicano way, doesn't want to acknowledge that he's having sex with a man. In a similar sense, nor does Scott in* My Own Private Idaho *fully embrace it. And, in fact, isn't Pepper in some ways the blueprint for Scott in an early version of the script you wrote for* Idaho?

GVS: I guess they're similar characters. I think the origins of *Mala Noche* and *My Own Private Idaho* were John Rechy's novel *City of Night,* which had characters who admitted to being street hustlers but not to being gay – there was something about taking money for sex that validated that. After Pepper spent the night with Walt [played by Tim

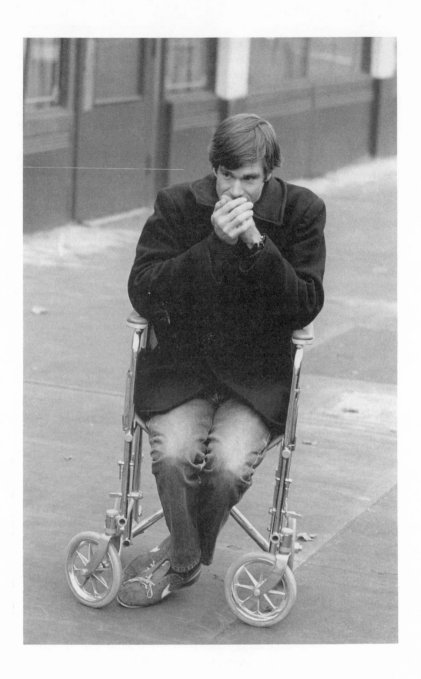

Streeter], he stole ten dollars. Certainly there was this whole machismo kind of thing going on, since he was from Mexico.

In Scott's case, in *My Own Private Idaho*, I was fashioning those characters after people that I had met in Portland who are street hustlers; the same things that were in the characters in John Rechy's book existed within them. I wanted to expose that side. I don't know if it came out of *Mala Noche*. I think it came out of the paradox of people having sex with someone of the same sex yet refusing the label that this gave them.

GF: *Isn't there a direct link between Pepper and Scott? You'd written a short story about the actor, Ray Monge, who played Pepper, and his cousin Little George, which became part of the* Idaho *script.*

GVS: Well, in fashioning *My Own Private Idaho*, there were a number of scripts that I was writing. The original script was written in the seventies when I was living in Hollywood. It was actually set on Hollywood Boulevard, but when I read *City of Night*, which was also set there, I realized that that was so much better than what I was writing. I stopped writing, and decided that either I'd do *City of Night* or else I shouldn't do this project.

Meanwhile, I had shot *Mala Noche* and eight years went by. Then I started writing again about these same street characters. Actually, when I was editing *Mala Noche*, I had met Mike, who became the sort of guide to the character of Mike in the film.

GF: *Was he a narcoleptic?*

GVS: No. But he smoked a lot of pot, and as a sort of defense mechanism, he would say he had forgotten something. You know, if you said, 'Why weren't you here when you said you'd be here?' or whatever, he'd say, 'Well, I don't remember that.' So it seemed like he had narcolepsy.

So I was writing this thing about Mike, who had a friend named Scott. In the script, I made him a rich kid, although he wasn't in reality. Although I think there were rich kids like that on the streets, I didn't fully know who he was until I saw Orson Welles's *Chimes at Midnight*.

Seeing that, I realized that Shakespeare's *Henry IV* plays had this gritty quality about them. They had the young Henry, Prince Hal, who is about to become king, slumming on the streets with his sidekick. The young Henry seemed to be Scott and the sidekick seemed to be Mike, so I adapted the Shakespeare story to modern Portland. It was called *In a Blue Funk* or *Minions of the Moon*; it had a lot of different titles. At that time I had, through *Mala Noche*, gotten an agent, and I showed the script to somebody at 20th Century-Fox who liked Shakespeare. Eventually we toned the Shakespeare down and made the language more modern. But at the time it was literally, from beginning to end, a restructuring of the *Henry IV* plays.

I was also working on this short story called *My Own Private Idaho* which I intended to film. It was about twenty-five pages long and about Ray and Little George. Ray was the guy who played Pepper in *Mala Noche* and Little George was his cousin. They were real people, but the characters that I was writing were like Mike and Scott. They were two Latino characters on the streets of Portland. Ray was eighteen, a street hustler, and Little George was a thirteen-year-old homeless kid with a dog. They went on the road in search of their parents, or some relative, and to a town in Spain that had the same last name as Ray's character. I don't think I had a town name in my story; I was trying to figure out what that was going to be. Ray was going to randomly look up somebody with his last name and assume that he was related, and the people in the town were going to think that they were American relatives. Then they were going to live in Spain until Ray fell in love with a girl and went off on honeymoon, leaving Little George behind with this dog. That's where that part of Scott and Mike's story came from in the film.

Then I had another script called *The Boys of Storytown*, or something like that, which had the Mike and Scott characters. That was the part of the story where they were on the street. In that, Mike has narcolepsy and keeps passing out, Scott has just come to town and runs into this German guy, Hans, who Mike had lived with for a while. In the movie he doesn't, but in one of these early scripts, he lived with Hans for half the film and they had this funny domestic relationship. Then he leaves Hans and goes back on the street, and there's a character named Bob . . . I don't remember what happened after that. It could have just been a half-written thing.

I wanted to make this film but it didn't really have a cohesive script. When *Drugstore Cowboy* happened, it took up my time for about a year and a half, after which I decided that I would refine *My Own Private Idaho* by combining these three scripts together, which I did while we were editing *Drugstore*. It combined the Ray–George characters with the Mike–Scott characters, and I threw the Shakespeare in the middle and bookended it with the other stories. I mixed it all together and used that as my structure. Finally, I hammered out the version which became *My Own Private Idaho*. By the time *Drugstore Cowboy* came out, it was finished and I declared it as my next project and that it was going to star the original Mike and that I had somebody, Rodney, who was going to play Scott.

You know, it's all kind of mixed up! Ray, in the story, was never really *Ray*, and Scott didn't necessarily come from Ray in *Mala Noche*. Everything was influencing everything else. I think that the tentatively non-gay hustler character is to be found in many places.

GF: *You seem to blur the notions of sexual identity purposely, as if labels like 'gay' and 'straight' aren't particularly helpful. Again, in* Even Cowgirls Get the Blues, *Sissy Hankshaw has sex with both men and women, but her sexual identity isn't really the issue.*

GVS: Well, I don't know. I guess all these stories are concerned with showing that. Walt in *Mala Noche* is always talking about it, asking, What does it mean? And then Sissy in Tom Robbins's novel is this pan-sexual character who finds delight in the sexuality of women, and that is presented as an OK thing. The characters in *My Own*

Private Idaho are literally blurred because their sexuality is a business as opposed to an emotion. They occupy a different space, I think, than Walt and Pepper and Sissy Hankshaw.

Those were just the projects that I was picking up at the time. I guess it reflects my own point of view, maybe artistically rather than politically.

GF: *Where did you come across James Fogle's unpublished novel* Drugstore Cowboy?

GVS: Through the Portland group of filmmakers, I had met Daniel Yost, whose brother Jack Yost had helped Penny Allen raise $125,000 for *Paydirt*, which was the film she made after *Property*. When I moved to Portland, I thought I could use a producer, and I asked Jack if he would raise the money for *Mala Noche*. He was half interested, but he was also cautious because he thought that Walt's novel wouldn't make such a good film. Dan Yost, a sportswriter who had become associated with the film consortium, had worked with Thomas E. Gaddis, who had written the book *The Birdman of Alcatraz*. In one of his classes, Gaddis had told Dan about James Fogle, who was a novelist in prison who couldn't really get his manuscripts around. By the time I showed up, these manuscripts had been sitting in Dan's cabinet for about seven or eight years and he had tried writing a screenplay from one of them, *Satan's Sandbox*. I actually liked that one better than *Drugstore Cowboy*. It was a prison triangle involving an effeminate black transvestite, Ivy, who ran a beauty parlour in prison, and two other inmates, Mike, unbelievably enough, and Ivy's former lover, Zitzer, who was a real guy. This was in San Quentin, where Fogle had spent time. Mike, who was about eighteen and had been thrown into prison for causing a traffic accident where two women were killed, falls in love with Ivy and they have this torrid semi-gay love affair, to the amusement of Zitzer. It was a comment on sexuality in prison, which has different rules from sexuality outside of prison.

I think Dan had originally shown it to me because it

made a connection with *Mala Noche*. Since I'd been out in Hollywood pitching *My Own Private Idaho*, he felt that I could pitch Fogle's manuscripts. So I started pitching them and then it became obvious that we needed to fashion scripts of them on spec.

GF: *Did you just write* Drugstore?

GVS: Both of them. Then eventually Avenue Pictures decided to produce *Drugstore Cowboy*.

GF: *Where does your affinity for street kids and junkies and hustlers come from and why do you seek to tell their stories? Is that in any way a reaction to your own middle-class upbringing?*

GVS: It's certainly very much apart from my own upbringing. I think it's that *Mala Noche, Drugstore Cowboy,* and *My Own Private Idaho* had settings that were unfamiliar enough to me that they seemed like fairytale land. Perhaps a need to tell a certain type of story that was set in a place that I didn't know anything about; adventure could be had because it's a land far away. In the case of *Mala Noche*, it was a land of transients and loggers and winos in a grocery on Skid Row. In *Drugstore Cowboy*, it was a land of holdup men and drug addicts. Then in *Idaho*, it was a land of homeless kids who sold themselves for money on the streets. All three of them are close to each other, but far away from the public, from the viewers, in the sense that *Star Wars* or pirate adventures are far away from them. It's a storyteller's technique to remove you from everyday life into a new area, so parables can be had.

GF: *The difference is that you are dealing with worlds that do exist and which are very harsh.*

GVS: So are space adventures and pirate adventures – probably more harsh.

GF: *In* Drugstore Cowboy, *you didn't attempt to romanticize the junkies or to judge them. The film came out right at the time of Nancy Reagan's 'Just Say No' campaign, but you removed yourself from that – and from IV-transmitted AIDS – by setting the film in the early seventies. You have*

described Drugstore Cowboy *as an anti-drug film. What's your take on it now?*

GVS: I think it was an anti-drug film, except it came from a book by a drug user as opposed to a drug non-user. That gave it a stronger voice in terms of the anti-drugs position, because a user knows what he's speaking about. One of the strengths of the film is that it's coming from the voice of somebody who lived that life. Ever since Fogle started dealing with drugs – he's in his fifties now – I think he's been caught in a trap that he can't get out of. Largely because of the film, I think, he was able to get out of prison but, over a year ago, he was arrested in a motel not unlike the one that's in the movie, in possession of a lot of drugs. As long as he was out of prison, he was in this other kind of prison. The whole experience is Pavlovian – he describes it as such in the book of *Drugstore Cowboy* and we show it in the movie. It's an insider's view as opposed to an outsider's view.

GF: *Clearly you didn't want the film to be preachy.*

GVS: I didn't think we needed to be. I didn't feel that we had to be obvious. All the things that the movie says, the book says, are said in the same way: 'Make up your own mind.'

I think that the movie can be hard for somebody who's just quit drugs. I don't think it helps them very much to watch *Drugstore Cowboy*. But then again, if they've just quit, they probably shouldn't go see a movie about drugs anyway. It's different for a person that quit a long time ago, while a person who's never used drugs can see from the film that it's not too much fun. So it can work as an anti-drug film.

GF: *William S. Burroughs plays* Drugstore Cowboy's *junkie priest and patron saint. You've also directed Burrough's* The Disciple of D.E. *and a film of him reading his poem 'Thanksgiving Prayer' against the backdrop of the American flag. Can you tell me a little bit about your fascination with Burroughs? I believe you began corresponding with him nearly twenty years ago.*

GVS: I was always interested in his style and his theories. I met him in 1975. I'd read *Naked Lunch*, which was a popular

college book in the sixties, and by 1975 he had written *The Ticket That Exploded* and *The Wild Boys* and I read those. *The Discipline of D.E.*, which was published in a collection of stories called *Exterminator*, wasn't really like any of his other stories. It wasn't as outrageous. It was a pretty matter-of-fact parody about discipline, about the art of self-control, but it was useful, too. It was really the first film that I made out of college, before *Alice In Hollywood*. I used the money that I had made doing sound on *Property* to make it. My parents lived in Connecticut and I was visiting New York City one Christmas and I found William's number in the phone book, so I just called him up and told him I wanted permission to direct a film based on his story, though I didn't have any money to option it. He said it sounded like a good project, so I asked him if I could come visit and he said I could after the holidays and I went into the city and met him. Things were really happening for him then because it was the beginning of the New York punk movement and he was reading his stuff in punk clubs and becoming associated with Patti Smith and others.

He said it would be OK for me to use his story, so I contacted his agent and made the film. It has made a little bit of money. William knew it wouldn't make much because he had made some short films himself with Antony Balch. Ten years later I worked on some records that used William's words and I contacted him again then; he was by then a much more public figure. Two or three years after that, when we were casting *Drugstore Cowboy*, I thought maybe he would be interested in playing Tom the Priest—and he was.

GF: *Did he write his own lines for* Drugstore Cowboy?

GVS: Yeah, James Graverholz and William wrote some things. They had some things that they wanted to do with Tom, and I allowed them to do that, to change the character a little bit.

GF: *In a technical sense, how did you achieve the hallucinogenic effects, the little filigree shapes that float in front of Bob's eyes when he's tripping?*

GVS: They were just little models that we rented or bought. We made them spin and shot them against a white wall and then double-exposed them like they would have done in the thirties. It was pretty simple. We didn't have very much money for special effects, so we did them on our own. One word for those scenes would be expositionary.

GF: *When you do shots like the magnified close-up of the printing on the light bulb in* Drugstore Cowboy *is that stuff that happens extemporaneously?*

GVS: No, I had done that sort of thing in *Mala Noche* and I was hoping to do it again in *Drugstore Cowboy*. We never had time during shooting so we did them while we were editing. We chose specific places in the film where those close-ups would appear and then we got props and actually shot them in the editing room. That light bulb was from the editing table lamp!

GF: *I don't know how you interpret that stuff, or if you even care to interpret it. To me it's like punctuation.*

GVS: A lot of people think it works well in the film because a drug addict might focus on something that small, a light bulb or a match or something like that, and just stare at it, which is true, actually. Maybe we were cueing off a sort of aesthetic that was working its way into the script from the book. It was a stylistic device that I'd been playing with since I started photographing objects in the sixties. I remember buying bellows for my camera so that I could shoot things extremely close up. In my high school year book in Portland there're two pages of photographs of things that are so close you can't really tell what they are. There are things in my other films that relate to visual motifs that I've used. For example, the barn crashing into the road in *Idaho* was a motif that I had painted pictures of for about ten years. Those things are just a way to shoot something that works well and which is an essential part of my style.

GF: *Do you allow yourself to improvise visually, to depart from the script when you're shooting, or is everything very carefully mapped out?*

GVS: We improvise things. Each film has a way of achieving

its own style, a path. *Mala Noche* was storyboarded and we stuck to the storyboards; I figured out what we were doing before we shot it. *Drugstore Cowboy* was much more of an ordeal because of the way it was shot and the size of the crew. Improvisation happened a lot more in that simply because I wasn't able to stick to my storyboards; I was only able to pick up things as we went. And then *Idaho* was not storyboarded at all. It was also shot without any shot list. On *Drugstore Cowboy* I had a shot list and I'd rehearse the scene and then decide in what order I was going to shoot what. On *Idaho* we *didn't* decide in what order we were going to shoot. We always shot the 'first' thing, whatever I decided it should be, and then I'd choose the second shot. We'd usually start wide and then go closer, because it's easier to light that way. Then the same thing happened on *Cowgirls*. We'd just sort of shoot the first shot first, and then because each scene tended to have its own logic, we'd know what to do next.

GF: *What about dialogue — do you allow actors to improvise or experiment with that?*

GVS: Yeah, they do a lot.

GF: *Do you rehearse each scene as it comes up, or do you rehearse the whole film first?*

GVS: I usually have a rehearsal period where we read through the script and do some scenes. But things are locked down when we actually shoot them, so it doesn't help to get too specific before that. Generally we rehearse on the set.

GF: *The best-known example is the fireside scene in Idaho, which was pretty much improvised by River Phoenix and Keanu Reeves.*

GVS: Yeah, they did that themselves. It was a short, three-page scene that River turned into more like an eight-page scene. He added a lot of things and changed the fabric of his character in that scene. He's a songwriter and he worked on it like he does one of his songs, which is very furiously. He had decided that that scene was his character's main scene and, with Keanu's permission, he wrote it out to say something that it wasn't already saying — that his character, Mike, has a crush on Scott and is unable to express it—which wasn't in the script at all. It was his explanation of his character.

GF: *How did you position yourself in order to get* My Own Private Idaho *made?*

GVS: I had basically finished the *Idaho* script eight months before *Drugstore* came out, but I hadn't had many meetings about it. When *Drugstore* started to get press, people in the industry started to talk about it in the same way they started talking about *Reservoir Dogs* last year. So I was this hot new filmmaker amongst this group of hot new filmmakers trying to get attention from the people who back films. Every time I met them, I told them I was going to do *My Own Private Idaho* and that it would only cost a million dollars. They would be very supportive and would want to read it, but after they read it they didn't really want to finance it.

GF: *Was that because of the gay content?*

GVS: It wasn't just the gay content; it was a lot of things. It was partly the way the script was written, which originally had lots of different-sized lettering, unlike a normal script. It was also short—about eighty pages—and the Shakespeare threw them. Basically everything. I think the very first sentence says Mike is getting a blow-job in a motel room. Then he's out on the road and he passes out, and the script talks about the house crashing into the road. It was very disjointed for the readers in Hollywood.

I was also pitching *Cowgirls* at the time and I had my first meeting with Mike Medavoy at Orion. He said it was interesting and about a year later, when he was with TriStar, he decided that I should get the script going. I eventually started working on it when we were editing *Idaho.*

Eventually, I got an offer of $2 million from an outside investor—we thought we had the money, although we didn't actually have it quite yet. At that time, Bruce Weber took a picture of me and the original Mike at the Shangri La in Santa Monica for *Interview* magazine. It was like a publicity stunt. I had bussed Mike down from Portland specifically for the picture, thinking Bruce would probably like the way he looked. So there's this picture of the two of us in front of this mirror, and Mike's hair is wet and he has no shirt on, and it says that he is going to star in *My Own Private Idaho.*

Right about then there was a mix-up between River Phoenix's agent and my producer, Laurie Parker, as to exactly what *My Own Private Idaho* was going to be, because there was another script, called *Revolver*, that somebody was offering River with my name attached. The agent didn't know why the producer of *My Own Private Idaho* didn't know about *Revolver*. She assumed that *My Own Private Idaho* was some sort of trick and she wouldn't let us speak to River. But somehow we found him and I talked to him about the project. Then I had a meeting with Keanu Reeves, who said he was looking for a low-budget film. I told him that it would be done up in Portland and that it would be a small thing, and he thought it was cool. I then went and spent half a day with River in Florida because he was having a hard time making up his mind. Suddenly there was this buzz about the film because all the producers in Hollywood who were trying to cast River and Keanu in their movies were getting the word that they were going to be in *My Own Private Idaho* and they wouldn't have the time to be in the other movies. All these people were coming up to me and congratulating me, even though River and Keanu hadn't committed yet. Finally, they did and that knocked the original choices, Mike and Rodney, into second-string. They were still in the film, but as different characters. We couldn't turn down the opportunity to work with these bigger names. Even then we put it off for nine months or so while River did *Dogfight.* By then, the guy with the money had disappeared, but Laurie shopped it around and got New Line involved. It was quite a saga.

GF: *Had you had to downscale the budget?*

GVS: Oh, no, it was bigger because the actors made it bigger. It was about $2.5 million.

GF: *The* Idaho *script that's published in this book is different in places from the film.*

GVS: It doesn't have the fireside scene that River reworked as it exists in the film. It's printed the way that it was originally written so you can see the difference. I don't see any point in just transcribing the film. The same with *Cowgirls*. In both cases the script we worked from was the one that's being published. It's valuable to be able to see how things changed during shooting. In *Cowgirls*, there're whole scenes that appear at the end of the script that are now at the beginning of the movie. There are scenes in the script that we shot, but didn't make it into the finished film.

GF: *When you wrote the* Henry IV *scenes for* Idaho, *did you actually go back to the text of the plays or was your reference point* Chimes at Midnight?

GVS: I tried to forget the Welles film because I didn't want to be plagiaristic or stylistically influenced by it, even though it had given me the idea. So I referred to the original Shakespeare. When *My Own Private Idaho* was shown at the Venice Biennale someone put together a comparative study of the Shakespeare scenes that I'd used and the same scenes from a different text of the play. I started to

realize that there were many different versions of
Shakespeare.

GF: *Kenneth Branagh's* Henry V *also imported the Falstaff scenes
from* Henry IV, Part I.

GVS: Yes, the flashbacks—we used some of the same scenes
actually.

GF: *Why did you cut down on the scenes with Jane Lightwork—
your version of Mistress Quickly—in the film?*

GVS: There were a couple of different characters that got
slimmed down because the Shakespeare scenes were
becoming like a movie within the movie. It was
interesting up to a point, but in the editing room we were
still trying to figure out whether or not it would fly.
There was a whole contingent of people at New Line—the
domestic distributors—who were totally against the
Shakespeare scenes and wanted us to cut them all out.
The foreign distributors wanted as much Shakespeare in
there as we could get. In the end, we cut out one long
scene between Scott and Bob [William Reichert], who are
Prince Hal and Falstaff, when they put on a play and
Falstaff does this mock-deposing of the king. It was nice,
but it went on too long.

GF: *I'm curious to know if you've been influenced by Derek
Jarman's Shakespeare films.*

GVS: No. But I was influenced by *The Last of England*, which
is Super-8 transferred to video, then manipulated on video
and converted back to 35mm; I did the same thing in *The
Discipline of D.E.* I liked the way Derek cut *The Last of
England* together, similarly the way he cut his videos for
the Pet Shop Boys and the Smiths. When I saw *The Last
of England*, I was reacting to something that he was doing
that I had originally been influenced by myself—the
underground filmmakers of the sixties. For example, you
can slow the camera down to two frames a second and
project it at that speed so it looks like a NASA space
film—click, click, click—or you can make your exposures
longer if you shoot in the dark or low-light situations; the
images blur out if you pan or zoom around so that they're
almost like stills. Derek was doing that kind of thing in

his Smiths videos and I was reinfluenced by those techniques when I did videos for the Red Hot Chili Peppers, for example. There are things you do with a Super-8 camera that you don't do with a bigger one.

GF: *In* Drugstore Cowboy *and* My Own Private Idaho, *you made very evocative use of time-lapse photography.*

GVS: Before I finished *Mala Noche*, I taught a time-lapse class. I had done a little time-lapse with Eric Edwards in *The Happy Organ*—a sunrise, going from dark to light, with clouds moving across the sky. Eric had always experimented with time-lapse still photography, like late-night exposures that go on for ten minutes or an hour. I think we even did some experiments in 16mm together. Then he started making these images on his own with an intervelometer he'd made. He sent us a bunch of them during the edit of *Drugstore Cowboy* and I wrote back and told him to shoot specific things that we used in the movie. Then, on *Idaho*, on his own, he was doing these time-lapse shots that weren't in the script and the producer was worried he was using up too much film, but we cut them in for the scenes when Mike blacks out. Before that, we'd make the screen go black but it wasn't working. So Eric's shots became really important as our way of showing an altered sense of time from Mike's perspective. Although Eric continued to shoot some time-lapse stuff during *Cowgirls*, this time we're sort of shying away from them because we've done it enough, I think.

GF: *Going back to* Idaho, *it's central theme is the search for family, specifically, Mike's quest for his mother and Scott's for a father-figure. The movie is dense with references to family. Even in that harrowing scene when Mike visits his brother—who also happens to be his father—you see in the trailer that the brother has all these family portraits from his mail-order photo business.*

GVS: All the stories that I have done so far have had some sort of family metaphor. In *Alice In Hollywood*, the girl falls in with a family of people on the street. In *Mala Noche*, Walt and Pepper form a couple that's more like a father-son relationship, and in *Drugstore Cowboy*, it's like a drug

family. In *Idaho*, it's a street family again with Bob as the father figure, but it's a displaced, temporary family. The film's about *why* Mike's on the street—because his real family didn't work. That comes directly from a number of people that I've known that live that kind of life; in every case, they came from some sort of problematic family situation. One of the kids who I filmed for the interviews in the cafe in *Idaho*, but who didn't make the final cut, was talking about how he had a motorcycle accident and his family was sued for a million dollars and he had to leave because they didn't have the money and blamed him.

In Scott's case, he has a very rigid family order which is cueing off of *Henry IV*. The reason Prince Hal is running around the villages around the castle is because it's his last chance to do that before he has to accept the responsibility of being king—the same with Scott as the mayor's son. Mike's family is cueing off of this Sam Shepard-like family that is eating away at itself. *Cowgirls* is about a girl who is a hitch-hiker, who has this wandering spirit and finds a family on a ranch, a family of women that she ends up staying with.

GF: *Where does all this come from? It is something that you just find affecting, or is it a personal obsession?*

GVS: It's probably a personal thing. Families are interesting stuff. The dynamics of whatever kind of family you have is an orientation that you apply to the outside world. Maybe it's just the most interesting thing that I know. Even the Harvey Milk project was about finding a new family, the Castro Street community being a family of like-minded men who had a new style of relating to one another and had sexual relationships with one another. This was a very clear bond in the new Castro Street of 1975. Almost everything that I have considered doing has some sort of family theme, but you could probably say that about a lot of films.

GF: *Are you aware of autobiographical content in your films?*

GVS: No, I'm not aware of it. I'm not being analytical. I just create everything intuitively. If you're too analytical, what you're doing probably ends up being too specific. I think it's different to the way a lot of people work. I think the more successful painters or photographers or filmmakers or poets sift a lot of different things into one, and aren't analytical and specific and conscious of what they are actually doing. If you have a need to be conscious of what you're doing, that can get in the way of a lot of things happening at the same time, limiting the number of ways that you can express yourself in one image. If you're taking a picture of something and you don't know why you like it, you can sit there for a long time and figure out why. It might take you weeks to figure out why that one image is important. But if you sat there and pre-decided why the image is important, you might never take a picture. You sort of have a hunch why you do something, you know? You see things happening as they are happening, and you might have one reason why you're focusing on that one particular image or action. But then there might be a whole lifetime of reasons why you're focusing on it—and hopefully you are producing images that have a lifetime of meaning in them.

GF: *I guess I was thinking specifically of Scott coming from the middle class, as you did yourself.*

GVS: Well, he's probably me. I can use my own background as an example for Scott's background, and I did sometimes with Keanu, too. Keanu grew up with a well-off background himself and used that when he was figuring out how to play the part. We tried to work out who Scott was. At times he was maybe both of us, Keanu and me. Whereas River had a different background than I had and related more to Mike.

Scott comes from a wealthy family and his father is mayor because Prince Hal came from royalty, and that was the closest thing I could find to royalty in Portland. I think the film might have suffered a little bit from that because there is a difference between being a king and being the mayor's son. The reason Scott's like he is is because of the Shakespeare, and the reason the Shakespeare is in the film is to transcend time, to show that those things have always happened, everywhere. That's why Mike and Scott end up with the boys in the piazza in Rome, which is just like the street scene in Portland.

GF: *Where did the image of the jumping salmon come from?*

GVS: It's a real north-western image. The Columbia river used to be filled with salmon and it's being depleted quite rapidly. The house I live in was built by a salmon canner and cook and I always thought that was a good omen.

GF: *The salmon are jumping upstream, aren't they?*

GVS: Yeah, they're going against the current. That's the central metaphor, in that Mike is essentially trying to find the place where he was conceived. He's also wearing a jacket that's a salmon-coloured pink. So he's the salmon, swimming against the current that is life, and trying to reach his roots, which is his brother. I don't mention it in the film, but the Columbia river runs from Idaho, and when the salmon swim, they swim towards Idaho. So when Mike and Scott are motorcycling from Portland to Idaho they're traveling in the same direction as the salmon. I only just thought of that!

Another thing that occurs to me is that America has a certain culture that's always reverting or trying to figure out where it came from. So we are always going back to the origins of different styles from the Renaissance through different movements in Europe in the 1800s and 1900s. As an American artist, maybe I am also swimming back to relate to some sort of European movement, where I came from, as opposed to American Indian art movements, for example.

One metaphor that was not in the *Idaho* rewrites, that we didn't work on in the final version of the script, was that the boys are supposed to be going toward their ethnic origins, which in their case would be Scotland or Ireland or England, and trying to find a family that had the same last name as they did. As I said before, that was in the original *My Own Private Idaho* story, where these two boys go to Spain, travelling to their ultimate origin, a town that has the same name as one of them.

GF: *Sex in your films is seldom consummated in live action, if at all. For example, in* Drugstore Cowboy, *Bob and Dianne are interrupted by the police when they're about to have sex. In* My Own Private Idaho, *you use montages of stills. Is it too easy an option to show an actual sex scene?*

GVS: I used the photos so that you could see what happened without getting too involved. You could understand it without having to go through a sex scene, which can sometimes be hard to watch and hard to get into – or get through. There's a filmmaker I like who did some still lifes with nudes; the actors were just frozen. That occurred to me as a way to present a sex scene without actually showing it, or the actors smoking in bed afterwards. It was written down that way in the script.

GF: *You referred just now to Native American art as something separate from your own origins, and yet I've noticed bits of American Indian culture cropping up in your films; not only in the character of Julian in* Cowgirls *but also in* Mala Noche *and* My Own Private Idaho, *particularly the Indian war chant that we hear when Mike and Scott are sitting by the fire.*

GVS: That's because they're travelling to Idaho, going through Indian territory. It also says 'Warning To Tourists: Do Not Laugh at the Natives' near the fire. I think that comes from the Warm Springs Indian Reservation in Oregon.

GF: *These things might also signify that there are more ancient rituals underpinning the modernism in your work. It also occurs to me that* Drugstore Cowboy *is a kind of Western.*

GVS: Well, all these stories are really modern Westerns because they're written in the West and take place there. River Phoenix was born in Madras, Oregon, which is right next to that Indian reservation; I didn't know until he told me and I thought it was an amazing coincidence. That road that he stands on in the film is about thirty minutes away from where he was born. His parents travelled from Oregon to California, nomadically, like neo-Westerners that have travelled from the East and come West. Walt Curtis's story in *Mala Noche* is a sort of Western –

Portland is a Western town. Only fifty years ago, Portland had dirt streets. The people that live there are descendants of the original pioneers and of the Indians; you see that very strongly in Ken Kesey's books. My ancestors went as far as Kentucky and settled there, then eventually my parents went to Portland. That kind of history is behind a lot of the characters in the films.

GF: *Finally, on* My Own Private Idaho, *the ending is ambivalent. Mike's lying in the road and someone drives up and takes him away. In the script it says it's Scott who picks him up, but in the film that's not clear. Also, you don't know whether this person is going to save him or hurt him.*

GVS: You're not supposed to know, really. It's like the end of *Drugstore Cowboy,* where people don't know whether Bob dies or survives. Some people have asked me who picks Mike up. In a way, it's either *you* who's the person picking him up or you're *him,* just being asleep. Or it's just a non-ending, and you assume he will go on in his quest. He's a character that has a hard time changing, so he's just going to go on like that forever–wandering and searching.

GF: *In* Even Cowgirls Get the Blues *is there a similar sense that Sissy–the consummate hitch-hiker–is trying to hitch a ride with us?*

GVS: You could look at it that way, though it's not really as pointed as the other films in terms of being told from the character's point of view. Sissy is more of a character apart from the audience's point of view. You are experiencing things along with her, but they're not necessarily told from her perspective. *Mala Noche, Drugstore Cowboy,* and *My Own Private Idaho* are definitely films that are told through the characters' eyes. Less so with Sissy. She's an object that you're watching as opposed to someone you're watching the world through.

GF: *When you came to write the script, how did you go about cutting your way through all of Tom Robbins's riffing on different mythologies and cultural allusions? It couldn't have been an easy novel to condense. What was your guiding principle?*

xlv

GVS: There are a lot of things that he just talks about, his own reveries, which are beside the things the characters are doing and talking about. Those went. I followed what the characters were saying, not the things Robbins speaks about.

GF: *Was it a hard job of adaptation?*

GVS: Just going by that rule, it was pretty easy.

GF: *But you did pull in quite a bit of visual minutiae from the book.*

GVS: Only in the descriptions of what things look like and so forth—not literally. There might be some things that I took out of Robbins's mouth and, if it was appropriate, put into one of the character's mouths, but it was pretty rare. There's a little bit of narration in the middle of the movie, and then there's a description of an inanimate object, a brown paper bag, which is from the book, but those are the only things I took directly. Robbins's discussion between the thumb and the brain, that whole thing about using the amoeba as a mascot for the novel— all that I had to leave out.

GF: *Did you invent a lot?*

GVS: No, because there was so much in the book that I had to edit out. It was really an editing job. It usually is when you adapt a novel. *Mala Noche, Drugstore Cowboy,* and then the Shakespeare scenes in *My Own Private Idaho* were all editing jobs and didn't involve too much creation. The non-Shakespeare parts in *Idaho* are the most creative parts of any script I've done. The novels I've adapted gave me really strict guideposts as to what I was doing.

GF: *Was it important for you to stay true to the spirit of Robbins's novel?*

GVS: Yes, and it's hard sometimes to stay true and not get lost. In the case of *Mala Noche,* Walt Curtis was around and he showed us some things that we could do that he remembered doing, that weren't in the book. Then, with *Drugstore Cowboy,* there were a couple of scenes in the book that we hadn't touched on in the script but which we include in the film; sometimes it's just a few lines.

xlvi

The same with *Cowgirls* where we shot an extra scene from the book, though it didn't make the final cut.

GF: *It was reported in the gossip column of the* New York Post *that you'd cut out a long scene involving the Keanu Reeves character, Julian.*

GVS: The problem was that Julian is only a passing character in the movie. In the novel, there's a whole engaged kind of life that Sissy has with Julian, who is a gentrified Mohawk Indian living in New York. He represents traditional marriage and she ends up marrying him and becoming dissatisfied with her life because she feels pinned down. All this is going on while she's hitch-hiking to the ranch and back again, and eventually he loses her. It was evident when I was writing the script that these were two different stories. There was one at the ranch with Bonanza Jellybean and there was one in New York with Julian. As time went by, we favoured the ranch instead of New York, and the way the script ended up Julian became a less important character.

What happened when we shot the movie was that Keanu found a section of the book that he thought was really interesting, and we worked on it and rehearsed and shot it. It was actually very nice in the movie, but it was a long scene that took away from Cissy's involvement with Jellybean at the ranch because it makes Julian's character larger. It was a close decision in the end. We wanted to keep it in and for a while we did, but eventually we took it out.

GF: *The novel talks a lot of philosophy. What aspect of that were you most keen to get across?*

GVS: I think my attraction to *Cowgirls* is that it's a kind of New Age novel. It was, as Robbins wrote it, setting up a new bunch of rules as to how to tell a story, and it mixed in a lot of different techniques on top of one another. That was what really struck me. It also plays with a couple of different genres, one of them being the romance novel. It seemed Robbins was using the form of the romance novel to write a new fiction. He has the lead character going in and out of different sexual situations to

create this very grand, *Gone with the Wind* type of journey. As she's a hitch-hiker, it could also be a road movie, which I think my other movies are, too, including *Mala Noche*, although I read *Cowgirls* before I read *Mala Noche* or considered any of the other movies. There were a lot of really exciting, unexpected storytelling elements that inspired me to turn *Cowgirls* into a script. It'd take too long to describe specifically what the message of the movie is because there's a lot of different characters who explain their philosophies of life and Sissy experiences each different one. Then she has her own philosophy, which is just to keep moving. I don't know if there is any one specific idea, except maybe 'time' itself, rhythm itself, is a kind of metaphor within the overall scheme of the movie. Time measured by travel, distance, practices; time measured by literal time, historical time, philosophical time, or religious time.

GF: *What were your feelings about the camp, over-the-top country-and-western ambiance of the novel?*

GVS: The campiness and the irreverent quality is, I think, a philosophy of life that comes from Robbins himself—like, don't take things too seriously.

GF: *Do you regard your film of* Cowgirls *as a kind of non-ideological feminist film, in the same way that* My Own Private Idaho *could be described as a non-ideological gay film?*

GVS: No, not really—they're almost opposite. Although *Idaho* has characters that are perhaps gay and perhaps not, I don't think it's specifically talking about homosexuality. The boys are making money from sex, usually with men, but the film doesn't have any kind of backbone that makes it a gay film as such; except that it was made by me. *Cowgirls* has a much more organized sort of agenda, presenting philosophies that are feminist. Maybe *Idaho* is a non-gay film made by a gay director and *Cowgirls* is a feminist film adapted from a book by a non-feminist or a non-female writer, Robbins, and also directed by a man: me. The philosophies and the discussions in *Cowgirls* are extremely pro-feminist or pro-female, and pro new life.

1

There're all kinds of things that go on within it that
address that.

GF: *Reading the script, I thought of it as an estrogen movie
because it repudiates feminine-hygiene sprays and celebrates
female juices in all their olfactory power.*

GVS: It's also part of those times, the seventies, when there was
an insistence on feminine hygiene. Body odours and
feminine odours, in particular, were to be covered up. At
the time, the Food and Drug Administration had found
problems with the hygienes that were being marketed.
This is why there's a character, the Countess, who owns a
feminine-hygiene company that has a staff of females who
are standing up and speaking for themselves, and
overthrowing the beauty ranch because of the products it's
making. The book is very hippie-esque in its point of
view: let the body smell the way it smells.

GF: *The Countess [John Hurt] is a misogynistic gay 'queen'. Are
you prepared for a certain amount of flak over the way he's
been depicted?*

GVS: I'm sure the Countess will cause some sort of an
outburst. Harvey Milk himself was accused of being a
misogynist by a large number of lesbians, and gay men
were often viewed as misogynistic towards the lesbian
community, even though they were after the same ends.
I'm prepared for some outrage, though – once again – the
tone of the film is: Don't take things too seriously. If
people want to take a caricature like that seriously, then
that's their problem. There's a famous Marcel Duchamp
quote that we use in Delores del Ruby's speech when she
addresses the cowgirls' extreme position in harbouring the
endangered whooping cranes as a ransom to allow them to
keep the ranch for themselves. She says: 'Playfulness
ceases to serve a purpose when it takes itself too
seriously.'

GF: *Would you describe* Cowgirls *as generally lighter in tone than
your other films?*

GVS: I think it's much lighter, though it's not quite as dreamy
as the others. There are things in the novel that are a lot

more fanciful and surrealistic than in the film, because we had to make them seem a little bit more real.

GF: *As in all your films, it has a ritual sacrifice in which someone dies. It was Pepper in* Mala Noche, *Nadine in* Drugstore Cowboy, *Scott's father and Bob in* My Own Private Idaho, *and now Bonanza Jellybean in* Even Cowgirls Get the Blues. *This would have obviously continued if you'd done the Harvey Milk film,* The Mayor of Castro Street.

GVS: Maybe in writing something where you are trying to explore the extremes of certain situations, sometimes the characters that die provoke the other characters that remain alive to change, and often it's meant to do that. In the film of *Mala Noche*, Pepper dies as a result of the immigration raid. Sometimes there are shoot-outs in those situations. In the novel, Pepper simply disappears; he was rounded up. I made him die to communicate the seriousness of the plight of migrant workers. They are more in danger on the Mexican border, obviously, than in Portland, Oregon, but that kind of death is more a reality to Johnny and Pepper than it is to the other people on the street in *Mala Noche*. In that particular film, that was something that I constructed. In the book, Walt didn't know whether he'd died or not until he resurfaced later.

In *Drugstore Cowboy*, Nadine's death is an emblematic drug death from an overdose, which was really common to the life that Fogle lived and an amalgamation of a lot of different things that had happened in his career as a robber and a junkie; it wasn't based on a specific person. In *Idaho*, the death of Scott's father echoes the death of the king in *Henry IV*, and it's mirrored by the death of Bob: Falstaff, too, dies in Shakespeare. So in that case, it came from the plays, and we used it to sum up the duality of the father figures. In *Cowgirls*, Jelly's death is the death of a traditional heroine, giving birth to the future of the rest of the cowgirls.

Harvey Milk's dying was one of the things that made them think about making that movie originally. Maybe it's similar to the deaths in the other films, but the way I would have done it would have been to show him as a martyr for the gay movement. He became stronger, and the movement became stronger, because of his assassination. I would have had him as a larger, straight-on hero than the characters in the other films who are more like anti-heroes.

GF: *You made* Cowgirls *for $8.5 million, by far and away your biggest budget. With all that money, did you find that you had to make adjustments in how you directed it?*

GVS: We had more time to do stuff; though we had a smaller crew than we did on *Drugstore Cowboy*. I haven't really run into the sort of thing that could have happened if I'd made the Harvey Milk film or in a situation where there's a lot of studio involvement.

GF: *Are you satisfied with the films you've made so far?*

GVS: I think in most cases I've been pretty surprised by the end result of the films. When you're working on them, you're always losing ground and gaining ground. You lose some things and gain some things when you're shooting. Then, when you're editing, you're not sure how it's going to turn out. *Alice In Hollywood* had been a really big disappointment; that just crushed me. But maybe it was good that the first one wasn't successful—I probably learned from that. So far I've been happy with the other films and the responses to them. Yeah, so far.

Foreword

Printed in this volume are the screenplays of *Even Cowgirls Get the Blues* and *My Own Private Idaho*, untouched and in their original form before filming began. We chose to publish them this way as opposed to printing a transcript of the finished movie so that one could better see the process of change that a project goes through before it reaches the audience. During shooting, the actors, cinematographers, and I would freely change things, adding scenes or shots, deleting them, and ad libbing lines or action.

On particular scene, the famous one around the campfire in *My Own Private Idaho*, was reworked by River Phoenix a great deal. River found this scene a pivotal point for his character and encouraged me to allow him to change his dialogue so he could express things that were not in the screenplay. I think you will find an interesting difference from the way the character of 'Mike' was written, and the direction in which River finally took him.

During the editing of the film, the editor and I mixed things around a great deal. This usually happens on my films, so that the end product differs greatly from the original intent. As the script of *Idaho* was forged, the ending had a variety of people picking 'Mike' up from the road as he lay unconscious. In the script printed here there is a specific person who picks him up, but in the film the identity of this person is hidden, so that viewers can make up their own ending.

Also during *Idaho*, Eric Edwards, one of our two cinematographers, had been shooting a lot of time-lapse views of mountains, clouds, roads, and such. Our producer, Laurie Parker, was having trouble justifying all the money that was being spent on the film stock that Eric had been using, but by the time the film was finished, I had fitted these shots into the movie to help River's character in his narcoleptic states. In the end, the time-lapse shots had become the secret meaning of the movie. They had become the *Private Idaho* of the title. However, this was only something that we came up with in the editing room, and so these shots and meanings are not in the screenplay.

The typeface of the original screenplays is a sort of patchwork I arrived at with my Apple computer. They were submitted this way and worked on by all departments in this form. The films of *Idaho* and *Cowgirls* began with unusual screenplays and everything that happened after that was a direct result of the way that they looked when people first read them. They are unconventional enough to have turned off a lot of people in the 'business' simply because those people were in the 'business' of conformity, as is most of Hollywood. I am not. To me this is extremely significant.

Gus Van Sant
June 1993

Even Cowgirls Get the Blues

a screenplay from the Tom Robbins novel by Gus Van Sant

fifth draft
July 6, 1992

Even Cowgirls Get the Blues was released in the Autumn of 1993. The cast includes:

SISSY HANKSHAW	Uma Thurman
BONANZA JELLYBEAN	Rain Pheonix
DELORES DEL RUBY	Lorraine Bracco
THE COUNTESS	John Hurt
MISS ADRIAN	Angie Dickinson
THE CHINK	Noriyuki 'Pat' Morita
JULIAN	Keanu Reeves

Directors of Photography	John Campbell
	Eric Alan Edwards
Editor	Curtiss Clayton
Production Designer	Missy Stewart
Costume Designer	Beatrix Aruna Pasztor
Music	k.d. lang and Ben Mink
Executive Producer	Gus Van Sant
Producer	Laurie Parker
Screenplay	Gus Van Sant
	Based on the novel by Tom Robbins
Director	Gus Van Sant

Produced by New Line Cinema

INT. CAVE NIGHT   1

There is a huge ancient hourglass made of animal skins, and acorns plop
through the waist of the hourglass one by one. It sits in a pool of water.
In the water swim EYELESS CATFISH in geometric patterns. An
underground stream feeds the pool of water and then flows into a huge
underground crevasse that on occasion emits a LOW RUMBLE.

INDIANS with torches surround the hourglass, which now we can see is in
a cave. And as soon as the acorns have finished passing through the
hourglass, a crew of Indians turn it on its opposite end. One of the Indians
appears to be JAPANESE.

ONE INDIAN stands at the wall of the cavern in front of a series of
symbolic carvings and scratches, with stone in hand he makes a few
hatchmarks, and keeps an eye on the CREVASSE.

THE CREVASSE RUMBLES once more, loosening a few chunks of rock from
the cave.

The earth begins to shake.

                        THE CHART KEEPER
                  She is restless tonight.

                        ANOTHER INDIAN
                  She dreams of loving.

                        STILL ANOTHER
                  She has the blues.

View of the chartkeeper's drawings. One is of a crane with a very long
neck. Another is a primitive drawing of a naked girl, who has long flowing
hair. She also has, pointed out from her sides, thumbs that are three times
normal human proportions. A MUSICAL CHORUS sounds at the sight of
this drawing of a girl with the thumbs. The chartkeeper puts the finishing
touches on the drawing.

And the song "Happy Birthday to You" strikes up on country and western guitar and polka-like accordian.

title

BIG   THUMBS

INT. RICHMOND VIRGINIA SUBURBAN HOME DAY.   ②

We see *CANDLES* burning on a cake. It is somebody's birthday. And there are six candles on the cake.

SISSY HANKSHAW is six years old.

Her DADDY and a visiting UNCLE, finishing their rendition of Happy Birthday, are staring down at Sissy and looking at her young THUMBS, WHICH ARE UNUSUALLY LARGE and twitch with a mind of their own.

She manages to blow out all six candles.

                    UNCLE
          Well, you're lucky that you don't suck 'em.

                    DADDY
          Sissy couldn't suck 'em, she'd need a mouth like a
          fish tank.

Sissy is negotiating a fork full of birthday cake, dropping it because of her thumbs.

                    UNCLE
                  (agrees)
          The poor little tyke might have a hard time finding
          herself a hubby. But as far as getting along in the
          world, it's a real blessing that Sissy's a girl-child.
          Lord, I reckon this youngun would never make a
          mechanic.

                    DADDY
          Nope, and not a brain surgeon, neither.

> UNCLE
> 'Course she'd do pretty good as a butcher. She
> could retire in two years on the overcharges alone.

Laughing, the men walk to the kitchen to fill their glasses. Sissy is left to feel sorry for herself in front of her cake.

> UNCLE O.S.
> One thing, that youngun would make one hell of a
> hitchhiker...

This startles Sissy. A new word that tinkles in her hed with a supernatural echo. Sissy looks at her thumbs.

> UNCLE O.S.
> ...if she was a boy, I mean.

INT. DOCTOR'S OFFICE   DAY   ③

Dr. Dreyfus looks over Sissy's thumbs.

> DR. DREYFUS
> She is, if I may speak frankly, somewhat of a
> medical oddity. Due to impaired dexterity, her life
> activities and career potentialities will be reduced.
> It could be worse. Bring her back to me if there
> ever is pain. Meanwhile, she will have to learn to
> live with them.

> MRS. HANKSHAW
> That she will. That she will. The Lord made them
> things big for a purpose. God don't never git tired
> of testing *our* kind. It's a punishment of some sort,
> for what I don't rightly know.
> (whimpering)
> Oh Doc, if a young man ever shows up here with, a
> young man with ugly fingers, you know, something
> similar, a similar case, Doc, would you please...

>   DR. DREYFUS
> Remember the words of the painter Paul Gauguin,
> dear lady. "The ugly may be beautiful, the pretty
> never." I don't suppose that means very much to
> you.

>   MRS. HANKSHAW
> It's a judgement. She's gotta bear the punishment.

Sissy beams serenely like a Christ figure.

INT. SCHOOL LIBRARY   DAY   ④

Sissy looks up "thumb" in the dictionary. It says:

>   the short, thick first or most preaxial digit of
>   the human hand, differing from the other
>   fingers by having two phalanges and greater
>   freedom of movement.

Sissy mouthing the words: "Greater freedom of movement."

EXT. ROAD DAY   ⑤

**Sissy very timidly ventures a pass with her gigantic right thumb in
the direction she is walking.**

She is passed by......BUT NO!

BRAKE LIGHTS! A Pontiac skids ever so slightly on the snowflakes. View
of the Pontiac insignia on the hood of the car.

Sissy runs, actually sweating, to its side. She peers in.

                                                             ⑥

OUTSIDE a palmist's trailer is a sign with a red silhouette of a hand.

Directly under the wrist where the watch band would be is written
MADAME ZOE.

Madam Zoe in kimono and wig lets Sissy and her mother in the door.

> MADAME ZOE
> I am the enlightened Madame Zoe.

⑦

Inside. Madame Zoe begins stubbing a cigarette in one of those
enlightened little ceramic ashtrays that are shaped like bedpans and
inscribed BUTTS. The trailer is cluttered, but not one knick-knack, chintz
curtain or chenille-covered armchair seems to have come from the Beyond.

> MADAME ZOE
> There is nothing about your past, present or future
> that your hands do not know, and there is nothing
> about your hands that Madame Zoe does not know.
> There is no hocus-pocus involved. I am a scientist,
> not a magician. I, Madame Zoe, chiromancer,
> lifelong student of the moldings and markings of
> the human hand. I, Madame Zoe, to whom no facet
> of your character or destiny is not readily revealed,
> I am prepared to...

Then she notices the thumbs.

> MADAME ZOE
> Jesus fucking Christ!

Mrs. Hankshaw and the fortune-teller turn pale and uncertain, while Sissy
recognizes with a faint smile that she is in command.

Sissy extends the thumbs as an ailing aborigine might extend his swollen
parts to a medical missionary. Sissy's mama draws a neatly folded five-
dollar bill from her change purse and extends it alongside her smiling
daughter's extremities.

Madame Zoe returns to her senses, and takes Sissy by the elbow to sit at a
Formica-topped table of undistinguished design.

Madam Zoe holds Sissy's hands while she appears to go into a trance.

She opens her eyes momentarily.

> MADAME ZOE
> You have a strong will. Will power and
> determination are indicated by the first phalanx.
> The second phalanx indicates reason and logic. You
> obviously have both in large supply. What's your
> name, dearie?

> SISSY
> Sissy.

> MADAME ZOE
> Hmmm. I'd say that you have an intelligent,
> kindly, somewhat artistic nature. However, Sissy,
> however, there is a heavy quality to the second
> phalanx- the phalanx of logic -
> that indicates a capacity for foolish or clownish
> behavior, a refusal to accept responsibility or to
> take things seriously and bent to be disrespectful
> of those who do. Your mama tells me that you're
> pretty well behaved and shy, but I'd watch out for
> signs of irrationality. All right?

She pulls her thumb to her breast.

> MADAME ZOE
> I guess the most important aspect of your thumbs
> is the, ahem, over all size. Uh, what was it , do you
> know, that caused...?

Mom speaks out from the couch she is sitting on

> MRS HANKSHAW
> Don't know; the doctors don't know...

> SISSY
> Just lucky I guess.

MADAME ZOE

Do you study history in school? Galileo, Descartes,
Newton? Lebinitz had very large thumbs;
Voltaire's were enormous, but, heh heh, just
pickles compared with yours.

SISSY

What about Crazy Horse?

MADAME ZOE

Crazy Horse? You mean the Indian? Nobody that
I've ever heard of ever troubled to study the paws
of savages. Well, I guess that about covers the
three-fifty charge....

Madame zoe lets go of Sissy's thumbs and wipes her hands on her kimono.

MRS. HANKSHAW

Husband.

Mrs. Hankshaw withdraws a bill from her rat-skin bag.

MADAME ZOE

Beg your pardon?

MRS. HANKSHAW

Husband. Will she find a husband?

MADAME ZOE

Oh, I see.

Madame Zoe takes Sissys hand and gives it the old tall-dark-stranger
squint.

MADAME ZOE

I see men in your life, honey. I also see women,
lots of women.

11

She raises her eyes to meet Sissy's looking for an admission of the "tendency", but there is no signal.

Mrs. Hankshaw does not approve.

> MADAME ZOE
> A husband, no doubt about it, though he is years away. There are children, too. Five, maybe six, but the husband is not the father. They will inherit your characteristics.

Mrs. Hankshaw, aghast, has heard plenty, and she ushers her daughter out of the trailer as if she were leading her from a burning cocktail lounge.

A title across the screen: (8)

Cowgirl Interlude
(Delores del Ruby)

EXT. BADLANDS DAY (9)

Views of vast vistas of arid grasslands, open and unmodulated, thirsty and exposed.

At the western edge of the DAKOTAS, the monotony of the landscape, now gradually tilting toward the Rockies, is interrupted by the *Bad*lands - sculptured canyons so deep and chaotic they can break a devil's heart.

Between the grasslands and the eerie badlands ruins, there lies a narrow band of humpy hills, green and pastoral. The hills are carpeted with mid-length prairie grass.

(10)

The Rubber Rose buildings are clustered at the badlands end at the base of a butte, higher, broader and longer than any in its vicinity, known as *Siwash Ridge.*

a sign over the entry of the ranch reads:

Welcome to the
Rubber Rose Ranch
(the largest all-girl
ranch in the west)

Delores del Ruby arrives at the Rubber Rose Ranch, carrying a whip at her side and batting an educated lash at the surrounding sights.

> DELORES
> I've traveled through the Yucatan with a circus,
> popping false eyelashes off a trained monkey with
> a bullwhip. When I ate peyote one night and had a
> vision. Niwetukame, the Mother Goddess, came to
> me on the back of a doe, hummingbirds sipping the
> tears she was shedding, crying 'Delores, you must
> lead my daughters against their natural enemy. You
> must come to the Rubber Rose Ranch and prepare
> for your mission, the details of which will be
> revealed to you in a third vision....' That night I
> whipped the shit ou' of my black lover and ran
> away. For a while I drove around, making a living
> selling peyote buttons to hippies, until I made my
> way here...

A snake crosses the road in front of her, and she takes her whip and whirls it around her head. The snake that is crawling across the dusty road that leads to the ranch is carrying a card under its forked tongue.

Delores snaps her whip at the snake and picks the card out of his mouth and lets it fly in the air.

Delores catches it......The card is the Queen of Spades.

EXT.   ROAD   DAY   (11)

Sissy is thirty years old now wearing a *trademark colored jumpsuit*. She
is saying these words still: "**Greater freedom of movement.**"

Sissy sticks out her thumb, even though there is no traffic.

A plane is flying overhead. Sissy hitches it; and the plane's flight path
curves with in response to her gesture.   A squirrel running by stops to
look. The bus on the other side of the road skids to a stop and two cars
coming her way stop as well.

INT. CAR DAY   (12)

The man driving looks over the back seat to the hitchiker behind him.

INT. BUS DAY   (13)

The bus driver does the same.

EXT. ROAD.   (14)

From the look of her Sissy is a very seasoned hitchhiker, and she turns
around relatively unimpressed with the fact that a car has stopped for her.

SISSY'S VIEW. The man driving is black-skinned, beret-topped and he has
four smiling gold teeth and six shiny brass saxaphones in the back seat. He
wears a gardenia in his lapel and tokes on a short joint.

>   SISSY
>   Going north?

>   MAN
>   You bet your raggedy white ass I am.

Sissy gets in.

He turns up the volume of his radio and rockets north.

INT. LINCOLN CONTINENTAL DAY   (15)

Sissy ventures into her pocket and pulls out a slice of cheese and offers it
to him. He now gets a better look at her unusual thumbs. They are
elegant, but large boned, and disproportionate. They are banana shaped
boats that makes it a little awkward to hold onto the cheese.

>   MAN
>   (taking an alarming interest in her thumbs)
>   Thanks.

>   SISSY
>   American Cheese. The king of road food.

He eats the cheese, and worries about the thumbs. He tokes on the joint
between his fingers.

>   MAN
>   Are you in show business?

>   SISSY
>   I was a successful model once.

>   MAN
>   For magazines?

>   SISSY
>   I was the Yoni Yum feminine-hygiene Dew girl
>   from 1965 to 1970, but got laid off.

>   MAN
>   So now you're bummin' around?

>   SISSY
>   Yep.

        MAN
Hitchhiking?

        SISSY
I'm the best.

        MAN
You're the best?

        SISSY
When I was younger, I hitchhiked one hundred
and twenty-seven hours without stopping, without
food or sleep, crossed the continent twice in six
days, cooled my thumbs in both oceans and caught
rides after midnight on unlighted highways.

        MAN
Whooee!

        SISSY
As I developed, however, I grew more concerned
with subtleties and nuances of style. Time in terms
of M.P.H. no longer interested me. I began to
hitchhike in something akin to geological time:
slow, ancient, vast. When I am really moving.
stopping car after car after car, moving so freely, so
clearly, so delicately that even the sex maniacs and
the cops can only blink and let me pass, then I
embody the rhythms of the universe. I am in a
state of grace.

The man listening to her takes another toke on his joint.

EXT. ROAD DAY   (16)

A view down the road of the Lincoln Continental going swiftly in its
direction.

CREDIT INTERLUDE featuring the song "Even Cowgirls Get the Blues" as sung by (an undetermined country or pop star like k. d. lang or Bob Dylan) in an old television Kine-scope piece of film like you might see on early 1950's television sets.

Between Sissy watching this image on old motel televisions, there are also IMAGES of roads, cars, trucks, highways, thumbs, gas stations and deserts gliding by in a flow of natural hitchhiking beauty.

EXT. POST OFFICE DAY   (17)

Sissy gets out of a large eighteen wheel truck and walks into a United States Post Office.

INT. POST OFFICE DAY   (18)

Sissy at the window picking up some mail, and opening a lavender colored letter that reeks of perfume, she is surprised to read this:

> ### *Sissy, Precious Being,*
>
> *How are you, my extraordinary one? I worry so. Next time you are near Manhattan, do ring me up. There is a man to whom I simply must introduce you. Thrill!!*
>
> ### *–The Countess*

Sissy looks at the envelope and return address.   Elaborately embossed is the Countess' logo...

INT. COUNTESS'S OFFICE   DAY   (20)

The elaborately embossed envelope is now being sealed...The Countess gives it a licking...Beside him is a young watercolorist named Julian.

> COUNTESS
> I will send this out to Sissy, she should get it in a
> week, and you will be able to meet her. When I

send a letter to Sissy, duplicates must be sent to
U.S. Post Office Boxes in LaConner, Taos, Pine
Ridge, Cherokee and that other place, for her to
pick up... Why she's probably out there right now
in Hibbing, Minnesota, or Deluth, Montana...hitching
her way across the country.

INT. TRUCKERS CAB NIGHT   (21)

Sissy is talking to a trucker as they pass down the road.

                    SISSY
          Right off, I don't remember how old I was when I
          found out I was part Indian. My mamma's family,
          a lot of them, had lived out West, in the Dakotas,
          and one of them had married a squaw. Siwash
          tribe. My pleasure in Indianhood and my passion
          for car travel might be incongruous if not mutually
          exclusive....
          ....After all, the first car that ever stopped for me
          had been named in honor of the great chief of the
          Ottawa: Pontiac......

In the distance, Sissy spies her destination. NEW YORK CITY.

                    SISSY
          NEW YORK CITY. It's still a helluva town....

EXT. OFFICE BUILDING DAY.   (22)

Sissy gets out of the truck and looks up at a large building.

INT. COUNTESS'S OFFICE DAY   (23)

                    COUNTESS
          Sit down dear, do sit down.

Sissy Hankshaw takes a seat. The Countess lifts a dusty decanter.

                    COUNTESS

Take a load off those lovely tootsies. Yes, sit right
down. Would you fancy some sherry?

The decanter is empty, a stiff fly lies feet up on it's lip.

> COUNTESS
> Shit O goodness, I'm all out of sherry; how about
> some Red Ripple?

He reaches into a midget refridgerator beside his desk and pulls out some
pop wine.

> COUNTESS
> You know what Red Ripple is don't you? It's Kool-Aid
> with a hard on. Tee Hee.

Sissy manages a polite smile. She looks at a heavily finger printed glass.

> COUNTESS
> (he toasts)
> To my own special Sissy. Cheers! And welcome. So
> my letter brought ya flying, eh? Where were you?
> Salt Lake City? La Conner? Well, I may have a
> little suprise for you. But first, tell me about
> yourself. It's been six months, hasn't it? In some
> circles that's half a year. How are you?

> SISSY
> Tired...

> COUNTESS
> That's the very first time in the eons that I've
> known you that I've ever heard you complain. And
> now you're tired, poor darling.

> SISSY
> A born freak can only go uphill.

> COUNTESS
> Freak, schmeek. Most of us are freaks in one way
> or another. Try being born a male Russian countess

into a white middle class Baptist family in
Mississippi and you'll see what I mean.

                    SISSY
I've always been proud of the way nature singled
me out. It's the people who have been deformed
by society I feel sorry for. I've been steady moving
for eleven years and some months. Maybe I
should rest up for a spell, I'm not as young as I
used to be.

                    COUNTESS
Shit O goodness, you won't be thirty for another year,
and you're more beautiful than ever.

                    SISSY
Does that mean you might have an assignment for
me?

The Countess taps his monocle with his cigarette holder. He looks on his
wall, and on a poster advertising a feminine hygene product, Yoni Yum
Dew Spray, stands Sissy Hankshaw, her thumbs neatly hidden, chopped off
by the borders of the photograph.

                    COUNTESS
You were the Yoni Yum girl from, let's see,
          (peruses the ad layouts on the wall)
    from nineteen sixty-eight through nineteen
seventy. You've always smelled so nice. Like a
little sister. The irony has just killed me. You, the
Dew Girl, one of the few girls who doesn't *need*
Dew. I loath the stink of females! They are so
sweet the way God made them, then they start
fooling around with men and soon they're stinking.
Like rotten mushrooms, like an excessively
chlorinated swimming pool, like a tuna fish's
retirement party. They *all* stink. From the Queen
of England to Bonanza Jellybean, they stink.

                    SISSY

Bonanza Jellybean?

COUNTESS
What? Oh yes. Tee-hee. Jellybean.

The Countess's jaw muscles calm down, his dentures ease into a samba...

COUNTESS
She's a young thing who works on my ranch. Real
name is Sally Jones or something wooden like that.
She's cute as a hot fudge taco, and, of course, it
takes verve to change one's name so charmingly.
But she stinks like a slut just the same.

SISSY
Your ranch?

COUNTESS
Oh my dear yes, I bought a little ranch out West,
sort of a tribute to the women of America who have
cooperated with me in eliminating their odor by
using my vaginal products, Dew spray mist and
Yoni Yum spray powder. A tax write-off, actually.

He looks out his window as a squirrel crosses Park Avenue.

COUNTESS
Sissy, Sissy, blushing bride, you can desist from
wearing paths in those forgotten highways. The
Countess has arranged a job for you. And what a
job...

SISSY
A job for me?

COUNTESS
I am once more about to make advertising history.
And only you, the original Yoni Yum/Dew Girl,

could possibly assist me.

The Countess hands Sissy an article that she reads clenched in her fist.

SISSY
The Food and Drug Administration said Wednesday
female deodorant sprays may cause such
harmful reactions as blisters, burns and rashes.
Although the FDA judges that the reported
reactions are not sufficient to justify removal of
these products from the market, they are sufficient
to warrant the proposed mandatory label warnings.

COUNTESS
Shit O dear, that's enough to make me asthmatic.
The nerve of those twits. What do they know about
female odor? Don't interrupt.
Here's my concept. My ranch out West? It's a
beauty ranch. Oh, it's got a few head of cattle for
atmosphere and tax purposes. But it's a beauty
ranch, a place where unhappy women - divorcees
and widows, mainly - can go to lose weight, remove
wrinkles, change their hair styles and pretty
themselves up for the next disappointment. My
ranch is named the Rubber Rose, after the Rubber
Rose douche bag, my own invention, and bless its
little red bladder, the most popular douche bag in
the world. So get this. It's on the migratory flight
path of the whooping cranes. The last flock of wild
whooping cranes left in existence. Well, these
cranes stop off at my little pond - Siwash Lake, it's
called - twice a year, autumn and spring, and spend
a few days each time, resting up, eating, doing
whatever whooping cranes do. I've never seen
them, understand, but I hear they're magnificent.
Very big specimens - I mean, huge mothers - and
white as snow, to coin a phrase, except for black
tips on their wings and tail feathers, and bright red
heads. Now, whooping cranes, in case you didn't
know it, are noted for their mating dance. It's just

the wildest show in nature. It's probably the
reason why birdwatching used to be so popular
with old maids and deacons. Picture these rare,
beautiful, gigantic birds in full dance - leaping six
feet off the mud, arching their backs, flapping their
wings, strutting low to the ground. Dears, it's
overwhelming. And picture the birds doing their
sex dance on TV. Right there on the home screen,
creation's most elaborate sex ritual - yet clean and
pure enough to suit the Pope. With lovely Sissy
Hankshaw in the foreground. In a white gown, red
hood attached, and big feathery sleeves trimmed in
black. In a very subdued imitation of the female
whooping crane, she dance/walks over to a large
nest in which there sits a can of Yoni Yum. And a
can of Dew. Off-camera, a string quartet is playing
Debussy. A sensuous voice is reading a few poetic
lines about courtship and love. Are you starting to
get it? Doesn't it make the hair on your neck stand
up and applaud? My very goodness gracious!
Grandiose, lyrical, erotic and Girl Scout-oriented;
you can't top it. I've hired a crew of experts from
Walt Disney Studios, the best wildlife
cinematographers around. You're my eternal
favorite. Princess Grace herself couldn't be better,
not even if she had your personality which she
doesn't; Anyway, dear, I'm out of photography now
and into water colors. Ah how circuitous
conversation is! We're back at the beginning. The
exact man I've wanted you to meet is my artist the
watercolorist.

Sissy dares a sip of Red Ripple.

                    SISSY
If you don't want me to pose for him, why do you
want me to meet him?

                    COUNTESS
Purely personal. I believe you might enjoy one another.

SISSY
But Countess...

COUNTESS
Now, now. Don't get exasperated. I realize that
you've always avoided all but the most
rudimentary involvements with men, and I might
add, you've been wise. Heterosexual relationships
seem to lead only to marriage. For men, marriage
is a matter of efficient logistics: The male gets his
food, bed, laundry, TV, pussy, offspring and
creature comforts all under one roof, where he
doesn't have to dissipate his psychic energy
thinking about them too much, then he is free to go
out and fight the battles of life, which is what
existance is all about. But for a woman marriage is
surrender.

The Countess refills his glass. The squirrel starts across Park Avenue again
but doesn't make it. The uniformed chauffer gets out of a limosine and
holds the crushed animal up where it can be seen by an elderly woman
passenger.

COUNTESS
But here you are, still a virgin - you *are* virginal
yet, aren't you?

SISSY
Why, yes, technically. Jack Kerouac and I came
awfully close, but he was afraid of me, I think...

COUNTESS
Yes, well, what I'm getting at is that there comes a
time when it is psychologically impossible for a
woman to lose her virginity. She can't wait too
long, you know. Now, there's no reason why you
must lose yours. I mean, just ponder it a bit,
that's all.

>   SISSY
>   (her brow spaghettied)
>   What makes you think this watercolorist and I
>   would develop a romantic reslationship?

>   COUNTESS
>   I can't be certain that you would. But what have
>   you got to lose?

>   SISSY
>   Well, okay. I'll try it. I don't see the point in it, but
>   I'll try it. Just for you. It's kind of silly, actually,
>   me going out with an artist in New York City.
>   However...

>   COUNTESS
>   Good, good, good...you'll enjoy it, you'll see. Julian is
>   a gentleman.

Suddenly the Countess swivels in his desk chair and leans forward.
Lowering his wine glass, he focuses directly, intensely into Sissy's blue
eyes. His smile widens.

>   COUNTESS
>   By the way, Sissy ...he's a full blooded Indian.

a title:

Cowgirl Interlude

INT. RUBBER ROSE OUTHOUSE DAY   (24)

The Outhouse Radio is playing "The Starving Armenians Polka" and
Bonanza Jellybean and Delores del Ruby are in the privy, caught in the
rain.

                    JELLY
Well, I'm not scared of a little rain.

                    DELORES
        Me neither.

                    JELLY
Might as well brave it.

                    DELORES
Right. I don't know about you but I'm sure not sweet
enough to melt.

Delores flicks her whip at a sweat bee that has taken refuge in the privy
and hits the photograph of Dale Evans upon which it has lit.

Jelly looks out the door of the outhouse across a cut green lawn to a
bunkhouse where we can see a gathering of other cowgirls.

There is a fly buzz and a distant polka yip. Way off horse lips flutter.

Bonanza spies a picture of Sissy Hankshaw, an advertisement for Yoni Yum
Dew Spray mist, on the privy wall.

                    JELLYBEAN
                (musing)
        Someday...... if that Sissy Hankshaw ever shows up
        here, I'm gonna teach her how to hypnotize a
        chicken. Chickens are the easiest critters on Earth
        to hypnotize. If you can look a chicken in the eyes
        for tens seconds, it's yours forever.

INT. BUNKHOUSE DAY   (25)

A meeting is in progression in the bunkhouse that morning. Mary is
addressing the group

MARY
I want to complain that some of the cowgirls have
been sleeping two to a bunk again, in violation of
the agreement that "crimes against nature" are to
be confined to the hayloft.

DEBBIE
I don't care who lay with whom or where or how,
but the moaners, groaners and screamers ought to
turn down their volume when others are trying to
sleep or meditate.

Some of the younger cowgirls blush.

BIG RED
I want to complain about the food around here! It's
rotten to the core.

A round of support from the other cowgirls in the form of cattle calls.

INT. OUTHOUSE DAY   (26)

Jelly and Delores are getting ready to run through the rain, when all of a
sudden, Jelly spies a barefoot cowgirl- it's Debbie - run across the yard in
her karate robe, jump on the Exercycle that is rusting in the weeds and
begin pumping the pedals furiously in the yammering rain.

DELORES
My sacred crocodile! She's flipped.

But in a minute, others follow Debbie, everyone of them, in fact; the entire
bunkhouse load of them, some thirty young cowgirls, squealing, giggling.
They slide and roll on the wet grass, push each other into the mud that is
forming by the corral fence, chase one another in and out of the thick folds
of rain draperies, stamp their cute feet in puddles and do bellyflops into
the overflowing horse trough.

The cowgirls frolic until, as suddenly as it has come, the rain goes away.

Play ceases. They are panting like puppies as they lean against one another or pick clods of mud from one another's hair.

> ELAINE
> I move that the meeting be adjourned.

> DEBBIE
> At the end of the endless game, there is friendship.

> HEATHER
> What the heck did she mean by that!

> JELLY
> Just that in Heaven all business is conducted this way.

INT. HOTEL LOBBY NIGHT (27)

In the lobby, the doors of an elevator open revealing Sissy inside wearing a buttoned up dress. Very formal looking for her.

There is Julian standing in the lobby. He turns and walks toward Sissy. He is wearing a rather formal looking plaid sport coat with blue cumberbund. He extends his hand to meet her, and (perhaps at the sight of Sissy's thumbs) Julian has an asthma attack, doubling over in front of her.

Sissy doesn't know whether to assist Julian or flee.

From the other side of the lobby, two WELL-GROOMED COUPLES, white, mid-thirties and upper middle class come to the rescue. The younger of the men, RUPERT, takes charge. He breaks an inhaler of dinephrine under Julian's nose.

> RUPERT
> We'd better take you home.

In the red of embarrassment, Julian looks more Indian than he had previously. Wheezing, he speaks:

> JULIAN

I beg your pardon. I've been enthralled with your
photographs for years. When the Countess hinted
that you might like to meet me - he never
explained why - I was ready to paint for him free
of charge. And now I had to go and spoil it.

EXT. STREET NIGHT   (28)

Rupert is helping Julian to the street. Rupert is a salesman for a publishing
house. His wife Carla, a homemaker, as they say. The other couple breaks
down into Howard and Marie Barth, both copywriters for an ad agency.

Howard hails a cab and Carla and Marie flutter around Sissy.

     MARIE
  This is dreadful.
   (lowering her voice confidentially)
  You know, asthma attacks are brought on by
  emotional stress. Poor Julian is so high strung. The
  excitement of meeting you - my dear, you look so
  stunning! - must have upset his chemical balance.

Carla nods. Everyone is piling into the taxi.

     RUPERT
  Come on, Sissy, don't be afraid of us.

     SISSY
  I've never ridden in a cab. The whole idea of
  paying for a ride makes my thumbs hurt.

Sissy is forced to suffer the indignity of riding in a vehicle she wasn't
responsible for flagging with her own thumbs.

     CARLA
  It'll be all right, dear. It isn't as serious as it
  sounds.

INT. CAB NIGHT   (29)

Carla starts to pat Sissy's hand, then decides to leave the thumbs to themselves.

The six of them are squeezed into the taxi. Sissy looks out the window of the taxi:

SISSY'S VIEW as the taxi stops at a light, she can see a newsstand headline on the front page of the New York *Daily News:*

THE CHINK SUMS IT UP, SAYS LIFE IS HARD IF YOU THINK IT'S HARD.

Ext. JULIAN'S APARTMENT NIGHT (30)

THE TAXI stops in front of Julian's building. It discharges its passengers.

INT. JULIAN'S APARTMENT NIGHT (31)

INSIDE Howard mixes Scotch and sodas, Rupert fills a syringe from a vial of aminophylline he has taken from its place behind a gelatin salad mold in the refrigerator. He gives Julian an injection.

> RUPERT
> There, that ought to beat them bronchial buggers into submission.

He turns to Sissy.

> RUPERT
> I was a medic in the Army. I really should have become a doctor. Sometimes, though, I feel that pushing books is a whole lot like pushing medicine. Think of books as pills. I have pills that cure ignorance and pills that cure boredom. I have pills to elevate moods and pills to open people's eyes to the awful truth...

CARLA
Too bad you don't have a pill for bullshit.

Carla smiles as if she were joking, but she'd said it tartly. Rupert glares and takes a big bite of Scotch.

HOWARD
(changing the subject)
Where do you live, Miss Hankshaw?

SISSY
I'm staying with the Countess.

HOWARD
I know, but where do you reside when you aren't visiting New York?

SISSY
I don't.

HOWARD
You *don't?*

SISSY
Well, no, I don't reside anywhere in particular. I just keep moving.

Everyone looks a bit astonished including the recumbent Julian.

HOWARD
A traveler, eh?

SISSY
You might say that, although I don't think of it as traveling.

CARLA
How *do* you think of it?

                    SISSY
          As moving.

                    CARLA
          Oh.

                    MARIE
          How...unusual...

                    HOWARD
          Mmmmm...

Rupert bites into his Scotch again. Julian issues a watery wheeze. Then, silence.

                    CARLA
          Rupert, before you get too engrossed in your
          research on Scotch as a cure for aging, don't you
          think you'd better phone Elaine's and cancel our
          dinner reservations?

Sissy leaves her chair and wanders about the apartment. Which is full of books and shelves.

                    RUPERT   (o.s.)
          What would we do without you, Carla? Without our
          little efficiency expert, Carla, everything would just
          go to hell. Carla is thinking about running for
          mayor next year, aren't you, Carla?

                    CARLA   (o.s.)
          Up yours, Herr Doktor Book Salesman. Will the
          demands of your medical practice allow you to call
          Elaine's or shall I?

                    MARIE   (o.s.)
          Oh let me do it.

Sissy is intriged by an antique here and an object d'art there, but she knows she is in an alien environment.

32

Sissy enters a bedroom There is a covered birdcage. She sits upon the bed
listening for a 'cheep' from the birds.

And gradually she reclines. Then turning her head to the side against the
bedspread:

> SISSY
> No Indian blankets...no Indian blankets...

And she blacks out. And the sound drifts away in waves, so there is only
the whistle of a distant wind through the mortar of the apartment
building...

...Until one by one, we see button necks freed. Soon Sissy can feel it.

Someone is undressing her.   In a voice webby with sleep she lifts her head
up, and sees Howard and Marie.

> SISSY
> Where are the others?

> HOWARD
> Oh, Rupert and Carla had a little hassle and went
> home.

> MARIE
> Julian fell asleep on the couch; we covered him up.

> HOWARD
> We thought that we should make you comfortable
> too.

Sissy thinks this is nice, but wonders, however, why they are both in their
underwear.

                     SISSY
         Yes, thanks...

Between the two of them, they have gotten Sissy out of her dress in no time. Sissy feels she should apologize for not having on a brassiere.

Marie slips out of her own brassiere and moves her bare bosom close to Sissy's.

                     MARIE
         Mine are fuller but yours are more perfectly
         shaped.

                     HOWARD
         Highly debatable. I'll wager they're the exact same
         size.

Howard cups his left hand about a Marie breast and his right about one of Sissy's. He weighs them in his palms, squeezes them the way an honest grocer squeezes excess water from a lettuce, and spreads his fingers to sample their circumference.

                     HOWARD
         Hmm. Yours *are* larger, Marie, but Miss
         Hankshaw's - Sissy's- are more firm. You'd think
         they would have started to droop; I mean, from not
         wearing a bra.

                     MARIE
         Howard! Watch your manners. You've made her
         blush. Here, Sissy, let *me* compare.

Marie seizes Sissy's free breast, quickly, like a monkey picking a fruit, rolling it about in her hungry little finger, rubbing it against her chin and cheeks...

...and...

...it was like her earlier days as a hitchhiker....nostalgic.....tropical plums.

                    SISSY
                  (in ecstacy)
        This place is finer than the place I live!

Like a disc jockey from Paradise, Howard flips Marie over and plays her B
side. Every now and then she reaches for Sissy to include her, but the laws
of physics insist on being obeyed.

Over and over Marie calls Sissy's name with half-closed eyes.

The Barths are really going at it, Marie yowling like a cat.

The POODLE in the kitchen begins to growl.

                    SISSY
        So this is what it's like...so this is what it's *really*
        like.

INT. LIVING ROOM NIGHT   (33)
Sissy bounces out of the bed and patters through the living room and
crawls under the cover with Julian. Julian stirs awake.

                    JULIAN
        Oh, Sissy. I am sorry about all the fuss.

Julian and Sissy embrace and go at it under the covers

But suddenly: Julian stops after a brief climax.

                    JULIAN
                  (with downcast eyes)
        I apologize.

Sissy cradles Julian and comforts him.

                    JULIAN
        It is the measure of Western Civilization that it can

encompass in harmony, balance off, as it were, such
divergent masterworks as A MIDSUMMER NIGHT'S
DREAM and THE AMERICAN DREAM, as the dome of
the Sistine Chapel and the ceiling of the Paris opera.

Sissy sits up, her eyes moping about the apartment, looking but not seeing
the macrame wallhangings, the volumes of Robert Frost.

                    JULIAN
            What's the matter?

After a while Sissy answers

                    SISSY
            I'm cold.

                    JULIAN
            Here. I'll turn down the air conditioner.

                    SISSY
            It's not the air conditioner that's making
            me cold. Nothing moves in here.
            Not even your birds.

Sissy gets out of bed and begins to dress.

                    JULIAN
            What are you doing?

                    SISSY
            Getting dressed. I've got to go.

                    JULIAN
            But I don't want you to leave. Please stay. We can go to
            dinner. I owe you a dinner. And tonight...we can...really
            make love.

                    SISSY
            I have to go, Julian.

> JULIAN
>
> Why? Why do you have to go?

> SISSY
> (somewhat frantic)
> My thumbs hurt. I've made a mistake. I've
> been negligent. I haven't exercised. I have to
> hitchhike a little bit every day, no
> matter what. It's like a musician practicing his scales.
> When I don't practice, my timing gets off, my
> thumbs get stiff and sore.

EXT. CITY DAWN   (34)

Sissy trembles while she kisses her thumbs.

> SISSY
> I will hitch with you, out where tall birds wade in a
> lake named for my Siwash kin. Out where Smokey
> the Bear lay down his shovel to romp with more
> playful beasts. Out where starlight has no enemies
> and the badland wind no friends. Out where the
> boogie stops and the woogie begins.

INT. TRUCK DAY   (35)

And Sissy is now traveling in a truck passing Fourteenth Street on her way
to the Geo. Washington Bridge.

View of that Bridge as the truck crosses it to New Jersey.

View of the wilds of New Jersey as Sissy travels to the West.

INT. COUNTESS' OFFICE   (36)

The Countess is on the phone.

> COUNTESS
> So she left town. Well, that shouldn't surprise you.
> Leaving town is what Sissy is all about. But tell me,
> how did she strike you?

Julian is on the other end of the phone.

> JULIAN
> Extraordinary!

> COUNTESS
> She's obviously that. Jesus! Which would
> you rather have, a million dollars or one of
> Sissy's thumbs full of pennies?

> JULIAN
> Oh, you! I'm not talking about her hands.
> They're difficult to ignore, I confess, but I'm
> speaking of her whole being. Her whole
> being is extraordinary. The way she talks,
> for example. She's so articulate.

> COUNTESS
> It's high time you realized, honey babe, that a
> woman doesn't have to give the best years
> of her life to Radcliffe or Smith in order to speak
> the English language.

> JULIAN
> Countess. I'm really in a dither. She's turned my head.

> COUNTESS
> Ninety degrees to the left, I hope. How does she
> feel about you?

> JULIAN
> I think she's disappointed that I'm not more, ah,
> sort of atavistic. She's got some naive, sentimental
> notions about Indians. I'm sure she liked me,
> though; but....then she left town.

> COUNTESS
> She always leaves town, you dummy. That doesn't
> mean anything. What about in bed? How does she

like it in bed?

Julian pauses for a very long moment.

> JULIAN
> How does she like what in bed?

> COUNTESS
> Like what?

The Countess' teeth chatter in his mouth.

> COUNTESS
> What do you think?

> JULIAN
> Well....er...

> COUNTESS
> Shit O dear, Julian. Do you mean to tell me you
> didn't get it on?

> JULIAN
> Oh, we didn't get it all the way on.

> COUNTESS
> Whose fault was that?

> JULIAN
> I suppose it was mine. Yes, it definitely was my fault.

> COUNTESS
> What do they do to you boys in those Ivy
> league schools, anyway? Strap you down and
> pump the Nature out of you? They can even press
> the last drop of Nature out of a Mohawk buck.
> Why, send a shaman or cannibal to Yale for four
> years and all he'd be fit for would be a desk in the
> military-industrial complex and a seat in the third

row at a Neil Simon comedy. Jesus H.M.S. Christ! If
Harvard or Princeton could get hold of the Chink
for a couple of semesters they'd turn him into a
candidate for the Bow Tie Wing of the Hall of
Wimps. Oogie boogie.

> JULIAN
>
> If we Ivy Leaguers aren't earthy enough to suit you
> hillbillies, at least we don't go around indulging in
> racist terms such as 'Chink.' Next thing I know,
> you'll be calling me 'chief.'

> COUNTESS
>
> Chink's the guy's name, for Christ's sake.

> JULIAN
>
> What guy?

> COUNTESS
>
> Aw, he's some old fart holyman who lives in the
> hills out West. Gives my ranch the creeps and the
> willies, too. But though he be old and dirty, he's
> alive, I'll bet, clear down to his toes. They don't
> have his juice in a jar in New Haven. Well I
> suppose that I'll have to write Sissy out on the
> road.

EXT. ROAD DAY   (37)

Sissy makes little puffs of dust as she walks.

From the direction of the ranch a VW Microbus is approaching. It is
painted with mandalas, lamaistic dorjes and symbols representing "the
clear light of the void."

When the Microbus draws alongside Sissy it stops. Inside are two men and
a woman. They are approximately twenty-four years old.

> WOMAN

Are you a pilgrim?

                    SISSY
No, I'm more of an Indian

The trio doesn't smile.
                    DRIVER
She means are you going to see the Chink?

                    SISSY
Oh, I may and I may not. But seeing him is not my
main objective out here.

                    DRIVER
That's good. Because he won't see you. We came
all the way from Minneapolis to see him and the
crazy bastard tried to stone us to death

                    OTHER MAN
Yeah, but I no longer believe that guy's a master.
He's just a dirty, uptight old mountain man. Why,
he pulled out his pecker and shook it at Barbara.
I'd stay away from there if I were you, lady.

Sissy walks on leaving the people in the bus arguing about whether the
Chink's rock-shower and pecker-wag actually had been intended as
spiritual messages.

EXT. ROAD DAY   (38)

WALKING down the long dirt road, Sissy stops to take a breather and sits
down on a log.

Sissy thinking and looking into the clouds.

Waves of grasses whisper her name: Sssssssss, Ssssssssssss Sisssy.

Meadowlarks squander their songs on her as she begins to squirm on the
log.

A Lincoln Continental *drives up suddenly.* Sissy barely has time to zip up.

The Cadillac stops in front of Sissy. A teenaged girl in a Stetson is at the wheel. The rear door of the limousine opens and a refined matronly voice calls from the void.

> MISS ADRIAN
> By any chance are you Sissy Hankshaw?

> SISSY
> Yes I am.

A chic middle-aged woman leans out of the car.

> MISS ADRIAN
> My goodness. Why didn't you telephone? Someone
> would have driven into Mottburg to pick you up.
> I'm Miss Adrian. From the ranch. The Countess
> wrote that I should expect you. Get in, won't you?
> You must be exhausted. Gloria, assist Miss
> Hankshaw with her luggage.

Gloria nods at Sissy amicably but doesn't make a move to help her.

Sissy swings her sack into the roomy vehicle. Before she gets in she flashes her thumb to hitch a ride.

The instant that Sissy shuts the door the cowgirl chauffer floors the Cadillac and it lurches away in a puff of dust.

INT. CADDY DAY   (39)

Sitting up after the bothersome lurch of the car.

> MISS ADRIAN
> Little twit.

(turns to Sissy)
You really ought to have phoned. We were just in
Mottburg escorting some guests to the afternoon
train.
   (sighs)
More guests leaving ahead of schedule. Three checked out today.
They decided to transfer to Elizabeth Arden's Maine
Chance spa in Phoenix, Arizona. It costs two
hundred and fifty dollars a week less at the Rubber
Rose, so why are our guests leaving and going to
Elizabeth Arden's?

Miss Adrian pushes a button that sends a partition glass between her
and the cowgirl driver. Gloria starts laughing silently on the other
side of the glass.

                    MISS ADRIAN
I'll tell you why, it's that plague of cowgirls.
They've gradually infiltrated every sector of our
program. The one named Debbie considers herself
an expert on exercising and diet. With Bonanza
Jellybean's permission and against my explicit
orders, she's been coercing the guests into trying
something called kundalini yoga. Do you know
what that is? It's trying to mentally force a serpent
of fire to crawl up your spinal column. Miss
Hankshaw, our guests can't comprehend kundalini
yoga, let alone do it. Yesterday, she ordered a new
cookbook by a Tibetan Negro, entitled *Third Eye in
the Kitchen: Himalayan Soul Food.* God knows what
that will be like. The little barbarians are
destroying everything that I've built, mocking all
that the company stands for. And there's a new
one, one they call del Ruby. She has the good will
of a scorpion. I've considered it prudent to avoid a
confrontation that might further upset the guests.
But now that the season is practically over - we
operate April through September - and the
Countess is finally coming...

EXT. RUBBER ROSE DAY   (40)

The limousine pulls up in the drive.

                    MISS ADRIAN'S VOICE
          Our Ranch has all the latest in modern facilities...

INT. BEAUTY RANCH   DAY   (41)

We see women having facials.

                    MISS ADRIAN'S VOICE
          We have a facial wing, and next to that is the Hair
          Barn...

INT. HAIR BARN DAY   (42)

Sissy is being given a tour by Miss Adrian.   A variety of hairdos are
witnessed.

                    MISS ADRIAN
          We have a team of fifteen hair experts from all
          over the world.

INT. EXERCISE ROOM   DAY   (43)

                    MISS ADRIAN
          And fanny flab flies off in this room at the rate of
          six hundred and seventy-five pounds a day...that's
          a lot of salted ham, Sissy....

INT. MAIN LODGE DAY   (43a)

Sissy and Miss Adrian walk through the lodge lobby, guests and
cowgirls are conducting a variety of activities:

A BIRD EXPERT projects slides of whooping cranes on the wall and is giving a lecture about the habits of the birds.

In the center of the room COWGIRL DEBBIE is leading a mixture of cowgirls and guests in a meditative chant as they reach high above their heads in a yoga exercise.

Miss Adrian stops in front of the registration desk and Sissy catches glimpses of the chaotic lobby.

> MISS ADRIAN
> Our special guest Miss Sissy Hankshaw is with us.

The receptionist hands Miss Adrian a key to Sissy's room.

A COWGIRL makes a face at Sissy as she walks by carrying a tray of herbal teas.

A representative of the film crew is being intimidated by a Cowgirl who is looking though his camera lenses and shaking them and listening to them like you would put a shell up to your ear to hear the ocean.

> COWGIRL
> Cool! We're going to make a movie!...

Another cowgirl, BIG RED, is lifting a piece of furniture and passes it to her accomplice.

> BIG RED
> Get rid of the furniture....it's too masculine...
> Get rid of all the furniture and use it for kindling!!!
> Break away from these pig-like chauvinist
> masculine influences....

Miss Adrian looks on helplessly....she grabs Sissy and leads her out of the lobby.

EXT. CORRAL DAY

Miss Adrian and Sissy walk out the back door of the Ranch and out near a corral, to the sound of gunfire.

> MISS ADRIAN
> O merciful Jesus! They're murdering the guests!

One of the FILM CREW MEMBERS is hanging out in the corral wearing a shiney jacket with DISNEY printed on the back.

Miss Adrian grabs him by the shoulders and shakes him.

> MISS ADRIAN
> Where are the guests?

> MAN
> Take it easy, lady. They went on a short ride with the cowgirls. Rode over the hill yonder. You're Miss Adrian, aren't you? We need to talk to you about the filming.

> MISS ADRIAN
> Not now, you fool, not now. Those crazed bitches have led innocent women out and are slaughtering them at this moment. We'll all be killed. Oh! Ohhh!

Another CAMERAMAN spits out a wad of chewing gum.

> CAMERAMAN
> There's a slaughter going on all right, but it's not the fat ladies that are getting it. Your hired hands are killing the cattle.

> MISS ADRIAN
> The cattle? They're killing the cows? All of them?

> CAMERAMAN
> (interrupted while putting a zoom lens on his camera)
> That's what they said, Miss Adrian.

A devilish young cowgirl is sitting on a fence nearby. Miss Adrian addresses her.

>   MISS ADRIAN
>   How dare you slaughter the Countess's cattle! What
>   is a ranch without cows?

>   COWGIRL
>   We're going to replace them with goats. Most of the
>   cattle are diseased and in pain. We're just putting
>   them out of their misery. According to Bon-an-za
>   Jellybean, the Rubber Rose is in-di-cat-ive of the
>   Countess's values. He has purchased a cheap weak
>   strain of cow to begin with and with improper
>   care....

>   MISS ADRIAN
>   Oh heavens! I don't want to hear what Bonanza
>   Jellybean has been telling you girls.... Come on
>   Sissy. I'll show you to your quarters.

(45)

AND THE SUN SETS OVER THE CANYON, THE HILLS AND SIWASH RIDGE
NEARBY.

(46)

THE CHINK, with his back to us looks down on the ranch from the ridge and
watches Miss Adrian lead Sissy into a small guest cottage on the ranch.

A DISTANT COYOTE HOWLS, AND A FEW SCATTERED GUNSHOTS ARE HEARD.

INT. RANCH COTTAGE   MORNING   (47)

Sissy stirs in a nicely appointed guest cottage.   A maid knocks on the door
and serves Sissy breakfast in bed.

>   MAID
>   Excuse me, Miss. Do you care for your breakfast now?

Sissy sits up and rubs her eyes.

                    SISSY
          Yeah. I feel a bit hungry.

The Maid puts the tray down, and the cloth that covers the food is lifted
away to reveal a shocking display of grease and calories.

A vase of prairie asters stands over a double-meat cheeseburger, a
package of Hostess Twinkies, a cold can of Dr. Pepper and a Three
Musketeers bar.

Sissy is delighted.

                    SISSY
          Road food. How did you know?

                    MAID
          Well it is a change of our usual grapefruit and
          melba toast, I'm sure.

Sissy notices a card. It reads:

```
+-----------------------------------------------+
|                                               |
|                                               |
|        Compliments of Bonanza Jellybean       |
|                                               |
|                                               |
+-----------------------------------------------+
```

                    SISSY
          Bonanza Jellybean....

                    MAID
          She will be up to see you directly.

Sissy devours her meal. Out her window she can see women on
exercycles, women doing jumping jacks and women in beauty parlors.

A FIST pounds on Sissy's door.

IN SAILS Jelly, a cowgirl so cute she makes Sissy blush just to look at her. She wears a tan Stetson with an aster pinned to it, a green satin shirt embroidered with rearing stallions snorting orange fire from their nostrils.

Her breasts bounce like dinner rolls that have gotten loaded on helium and, between red tinged cheeks, where more baby fat is taking its time maturing, she has a little smile that can cause minerals and plastics to remember their ancient animate connections.

Jelly grasps Sissy's elbow and sits on the side of the bed.

> JELLY
> Welcome, podner. By God, it's great to have you here. It's an honor. Sorry I took so long getting to you, but we've had a mess of hard work these past few days - and a heap of *planning* to do.

> SISSY
> Er, you seem to know who I am, and maybe even what I am. Thanks for the breakfast.

> JELLY
> Oh, I know about Sissy Hankshaw, all right. I've done a little hitchhiking myself. Ah shucks, that's like telling Annie Oakley you're a sharpshooter because you once knocked a tomato can off a stump with a fieldstone.   I 'd heard tales about you from people I'd meet in jail cells and truckstops. I heard about your, uh, your, ah, your wonderful thumbs, and I heard how you were Jack Kerouac's girl friend...

Sissy sets her tray on the bedside table.

> SISSY
> No, I'm afraid that part isn't true. Jack was in awe of me and tracked me down. We spent a night talking and hugging in a corn field, but he was hardly my lover. Besides, I always travel alone.

JELLY

Well, that doesn't matter; that part never interested
me anyway. The beatnicks were before my time,
and I never got anything outta the hippies but bad
dope, clichés and the clap.   But the example of
your life helped me in my struggle to be a cowgirl.

The guests are huffing and puffing in between the pauses in conversaion,
in the background through the window in Sissy's room.

SISSY

Tell me about it.

JELLY

About...

SISSY

About being a cowgirl. What's it all about? When
you say the word you make it sound like it was
painted in radium on the side of a pearl.

JELLY

Cowgirls exist as an image. A fairly common image.
The *idea* of cowgirls especially for little girls
prevails in our culture. Therefore, it seems to me,
the *existence* of cowgirls should prevail.
Otherwise, they're being fooled.   In the Rodeo Hall
of Fame in Oklahoma City there are just two
cowgirls. Two.   And both of 'em are trick-riders.
Trick-riding is what cowgirls have almost always
done in rodeos. Our society sure likes to see its
unconventional women do tricks. That's what
prostitutes call it, you know: 'tricking.'

Jelly lays her hand atop the oval mound Sissy's thumb makes under the
covers.

SISSY

You're political, then?

> JELLY

No, ma'am. No way. There's girls on the Rubber
Rose who *are* political, but I don't share their
views. I got no cowgirl ideology to expound.
"Politics is for people who have a passion for
changing life but lack a passion for living it."

There is a moment when the two girls feel something between each other.

> JELLY

Did that last comment sound too profound to be
coming outta my mouth? It's not original. It's
something I picked up from the Chink.

> SISSY

Really? The Chink, huh? I've gathered that you
sometimes speak with him. What else have you
learned from the Chink?

> JELLY

Learned from the Chink? Oh my. Ha ha. That's
hard to say. We mostly....Uh, a lot of his talk is
pretty goofy.

Jelly pauses.

> JELLY

Oh yeah, now that I think of it, the Chink taught me
something about cowgirls. Did you realize that
cowgirls have been around for many centuries?
Long before America. In ancient India the care of
the cattle was always left up to young women they
called *gopis*. Being alone with the cows all the time,
the *gopis* got awfully horny, just like we do here.
Every gopi was in love with Krishna, a good-looking
young god who played the flute like it was going
out of style When the moon was full, this Krishna
would play his flute by a river and call the *gopis* to
him. Then he would multiply himself sixteen

thousand times - one for each *gopi* - and make
love to each one the way she most desired. There they
were, sixteen thousand *gopis* balling Krishna on the
river bank, and the energy of their merging was so
great that it created a huge oneness, a total union of
love, and it was God. Wow! Quite a picture, huh?

Sissy's thumb twitches. Jelly swallows hard. They gaze into each other's
eyes.

A WHISTLE pierces the sunlight outside the window.

> JELLY
> That couldn't be Krishna, could it? A bit shrill for a
> flute. Just our rotten luck.

Jelly walks to the window and exchanges hand signals with someone
outside.

> JELLY
> Gotta run now. Delores says I'm needed.
> Somebody's here. Maybe it's the Countess.

Jelly spins her six-shooter in her kewpie fingers.

> JELLY
> Sissy, cowgirl history is about to be made. I'm
> damn glad you're here to witness it.

She holsters her gun and blows Sissy a kiss, then is gone out the door.

Sissy hops out of bed and from the window she can see cowgirls gathering
in a circle. Someone or something is in the center of the circle.

Sissy zips herself into a red jumpsuit and hurries outside.

EXT. CORRAL DAY

(48)

What was in the center of the circle was a goat. Debbie was scratching the animal's ears. She was hugging it.

> KYM
> It's cute. Way cuter than a cow.

> DEBBIE
> Goats are always testing you. They're like Zen masters. They can tell instantly if you're faking your feelings. So they play games with you to keep you true. People should go to goats instead of psychiatrists.

> GLORIA
> It's so loving.

Gloria cuts in on Debbie and gives the beast a hug.

> HEATHER
> Look at those playfully wise eyes.

> GLORIA
> Ooo! It licked me!

> JELLY
> More and more people are discovering that cow's milk isn't fit for human consumption. Billy West says if we can produce enough goat's milk on the ranch to make it worth his while, he'll run it into Fargo regularly.

She pauses and looks around the group in the circle.

> DELORES
> I'm aware that Tad Lucas rode broncs until her ninth month, but I don't think pregnant cowgirls are going to be any asset on this ranch. I hope you itchy clits who are sneaking down to the lake every

night are taking precautions. It's bad enough
we've got cranes coming; we don't need storks. I
feel that those filmmakers should be removed from
the Rubber Rose as soon as possible. Men can cause
nothing but trouble here. I also feel that our guest
(she nods at Sissy) should be excused while we
discuss this matter futher.

Hurt, Sissy leaves the group,

EXT. RANCH DAY   (49)

Views of Sissy in her Whooping crane outfit dancing to Debussy in
front of the Disney film crew. The documentary being directed by an
effusive Frenchman.

View of the camera crew training their long telephoto lenses on Siwash
Lake. They all seem to be wearing the same trademark satin baseball
jackets with one logo or another on their backs.

(50)

Another view of the lake, from above, from the Chink's point of view and
our first view of THE CHINK. The Chink spies Sissy and Jelly coming over a
ridge.

(51)

We cannot hear them at first, but Sissy and Jelly are talking.

> JELLY
> ......Delores zonks out on peyote at least once a week,
> but so far her Third Vision hasn't happened.
> Niwetükame, the Mother Goddess has not gotten
> back in touch with her. Meanwhile she and Debbie
> are rivaling each other like a couple of crosstown
> high schools. Tension. Cowgirl tension! What a
> drag.

> SISSY
> What is Debbie's position?

JELLY

Debbie says that if women are to take charge again,
they must do it in the feminine way; they mustn't
resort to aggressive and violent masculine methods.
She says it is up to women to show themselves
better than men, to love men, set good examples
for them and guide them tenderly toward the New
Age. She's a real dreamer, that Debbie-dear.

SISSY

You don't agree with Debbie, then?

JELLY

I wouldn't say that. I expect she's right, ultimately.
But I'm with Delores when it comes to fighting for
what's mine. I can't understand why Delores is so
uptight about the Chink; he could probably teach
her a thing or two. Ee! That grass tickles, doesn't
it? God knows I love women, but nothing can take
the place of a man that fits. Still this is cowgirl
territory and I'll stand with Delores and fight any
bastards who might deny it. I guess I've always
been a scrapper. Look. This scar. Only twelve
years old and I was felled by a silver bullet.

Jelly takes Sissy's hand, carefully avoiding the thumbs and helps her feel
the depression in her belly. The depression is a dimple, like another navel.

AFTER A HUNGRY STILLNESS, like intermission at a wolf dance, rhythms
are established. Jelly and Sissy are socked into one another now, and they
arch and push and corkscrew and jackknife softly but with pronounced
cadence.

Everything becomes scrambled. They rock each other in cradles of sweat
and saliva, until we can see nothing.

Noisy breaths buck out of Sissy: "Jelly, Jelly" but she can't hear Sissy
because she is screaming. Hysterical from the scalding hot softness of girl-
love.

EXT. HILLTOP DAY ⑤②

The Chink looks on from the hilltop above indifferently.

EXT. FIELD DAY ⑤③

Sissy and Jelly are riding on the back of a horse.

A WHOOPING CRANE is spied by Sissy as she rides on the back of Jellybean's horse back to the ranch. Delores and Big Red hurry to meet them.

> DELORES
> He's here.

Sure enough across the yard, in the midst of the low-cal barbecue in progress, monocle reflecting sunlight, cigarette holder stabbing the air, stands the Countess.

> DELORES
> Look at him. Perverse as a pink pickle

> BIG RED
> Sick as a vice squad.

> DELORES
> He's in a snit. He wants to see you right after the barbecue.

Jellybean chuckles sardonically and dismounts.

> JELLY
> Get the girls. He's gonna see me right now.

Sissy, confused, and loyalties torn in the face of an impending revolution, leaves the corral and

SLIPS INSIDE THROUGH THE KITCHEN ⑤④

DOWN THE HALL (55)

(56)

ENTERING HER ROOM, SHE LOCKS HERSELF IN. As she locks the latch she hears Jelly's voice.

INT RANCH OFFICE DAY (57)
Jelly has taken over the ranch loudspeaker system and is giving an ultimatum.

> JELLY
> Any of you ladies who would like to join us, you're welcome to stay on as a full working podner at the Rubber Rose. Rest of you get packed - and I mean now. You've got fifteen minutes to move your lard asses off this ranch.

INSIDE THE EXERCISE ROOM (58)

Women are reacting to the demands.

INSIDE THE GREENHOUSE (59)

Some women are taking up trowels and brooms as weapons.

INSIDE THE KITCHEN (60)

The help is joining the revolt.

INSIDE THE HALLWAY (61)

Other women are running for their lives.

INSIDE SISSY'S ROOM (62)

She hears the screen door screech open and a chaos of footsteps in the hall. She goes to her window. And she can see, partially cut off by the corner of the building, Miss Adrian screaming.

>   MISS ADRIAN
>   You will all be rounded up and sent to prison if you
>   take this any farther!   This is *not* your ranch!!!!

EXT. THE FRONT YARD OF THE RUBBER ROSE   (63)

The Countess seems to be taking it slowly, and calmly smoking a French
cigarette. He observes the fighting among them with amusement.

>   COUNTESS
>   You pathetic little cutesy-poos. Do you actually
>   suppose this exhibition of childlike melodrama is
>   advancing the cause of freedom?

>   JELLY
>   You owe us this here ranch, as a token payment for
>   your disgusting exploitations

>   THE COUNTESS
>   (tranquilly)
>   Then take it.

>   JELLY
>   Go for it, girls!

The hands, who carry axes, picks, pitchforks and shovels, retreat. The
Countess, still grinning, reaches for an hors d'oeuvre and subjects his
cigarette to a measured, self-assured puff.

>   MISS ADRIAN
>   (shaking her fist)
>   Go to your bunkhouse and remain there!

INT. ROOMS   (64)
The guests are hurriedly packing their things.

INT. SISSY'S ROOM   (65)

She looks on.

EXT. FRONT YARD

When the revolutionaries have retreated about thirty yards, they stop. With astonishing rapidity, they unbuckle unbutton and unzip and step out of their jeans and underpants. Then, nude from the waist down, thatched pubises thrust forward, up front and leading the way, they begin to advance.

The Countess's grin goes down his throat like bathwater down a drain.

> GLORIA
> Better reach for your spray cans!

> JELLY
> Not one of these pussies has been washed in a
> week!

Rather pale, his nose twitching, the Countess drops the caviar canapé he has been holding.

ON COME THE COWGIRLS, pelvises pumping, laying down what the trembling Countess believes to be a devastating barrage of musk.

Miss Adrian, lost in her own hysteria, charges. A barbeque fork she hurls draws blood from Heather's eyebrow.

Quick as a frog's tongue, Delores's whip cracks. It's lash curls around the ranch manager's ankles, pulling her feet from under her. She hits the sod in a jangle of jewelry and expulsion of breath.

A Molotov cocktail thrown by Big Red says hello to the sexual reconditioning building. Within seconds, the structure is blazing.

INT. MAIN HOUSE.

THE BARE-ASSED COWGIRLS storm into the beauty parlor and exercise rooms.

SOUNDS OF breaking glass and wood splintering. The air is singing with cries of "Wahoo," Yippee," "Let 'er buck" and "The vagina is a self-cleaning organ."

INT. KITCHEN (68)

SISSY flees the house as she hunkers down out the back door.

EXT. CROQUET COURT (69)

Sissy running across it. She passes the pool, and falls in. Climbing out, wet, scared, she runs to the base of Siwash Ridge and southward along the mountain's foot.

(70)

EVENTUALLY Sissy comes to a place where the juniper bushes are broken to reveal a crude path beginning a steep ascent. Sissy decides to climb up it.

She shoulders her way through low, slivery boughs.

Approximately halfway up the ridge she rests on a flat rock from which she can look down on the...

BURNING RUBBER ROSE smoking away, distant yahoos and carryings on can be heard. Horses whinney in the corral. A few gunshots are thrown into the soundtrack if things aren't lively enough.

MISS ADRIAN'S CADILLAC, **ON FIRE,** roars out of the drive.

Sissy looks up to the quiet mountain. Pauses. Then she looks back to the chaos below.

THE CINEMATOGRAPHERS' RENTED CONVERTABLE AND THEIR EQUIPMENT VAN drive away.

Sissy sits and wonders. The sun is setting on the horizon, mixing well with the firelight that the Rubber Rose is giving off.

BUT SHE is aware of something watching her. Looking about she sees nothing.

VIEW of an empty trail.

VIEW OF a quivering bush.

Sissy turns to the sound of the CHINK.

> CHINK
> Ha ha ho ho hee hee.

AND THERE HE IS. Standing only ten yards away.

The Chink's problem is that he <u>looks</u> like he rolled out of a Zen scroll, as if he says "presto" a lot, knows the meaning of lightning and the origin of dreams. He LOOKS as if he drinks dew and fucks snakes.

Sissy and the Chink scrutinize one another with mutual fascination.

> CHINK
> Ha ha ho ho and hee hee.

Sissy is just about to speak, but before she does

THE CHINK whirls, and scampers up the mountainside.

> SISSY
> Wait!

Warily he stops and turns, poised to flee again.

Sissy smiles.

SHE RAISES her ripe right thumb. And jerking it and swooshing it, she hitchhikes the Chink and his mountain.

THERE HE STANDS where Sissy's thumbs have stopped him. The Chink wears the wary look of a wild animal. He's not going to stay stopped long.   It is Sissy's move.

> SISSY
>
> Well, aren't you going to shake your whanger at me?

The Chink pauses for a moment, then he slaps his thighs and giggles hysterically. Ha has, ho hos and hee hees squirt out of his nose and through the gaps in his teeth.

> CHINK
> (laughter dies a nervous chipmunk death)
> Follow me. I'll fix you supper.

THE TWO doggedly walk up the steep trail.

> SISSY
> I'm a friend of Bonanza Jellybean's.

> CHINK
> I know who you are.

> SISSY
> Oh? Well, there's been some trouble on the ranch. I came up here to get out of the way. It's so dark now I doubt if I could find my way back down. If you could help...

> CHINK
> (voice that wears no pants)
> Save your breath for the climb.

SISSY takes another look at the Rubber Rose, which is now quiet. We can hear faintly a distant popping of washcloths and girlish laughter.

THEY make their way into a depression at the top of the mountain down a ladder of sticks.

THE CHINK lights a large fire in the middle of the depression.

HE puts a kettle of stew over the fire, and begins to roast yams.

THE CHINK'S FACE as the fire dances off it.

A CAN OF CHUNG KING water chestnuts is opened.

CUT TO: Sissy and the Chink eating supper on a rough wooden bench.

AND AS THEY FINISH, the Chink goes into a cave and returns with a tiny peppermint-stripped plastic transistor radio. He switches it on and the silence is broken by "The Happy Hour Polka."

Still clutching the radio in one hand, the Chink hops into the wheel of firelight and begins to dance.

Sissy walks around the fire watching the old geezer heel and toe, skip and hop. He flings his bones; he flings his beard.

> CHINK
> Yip! Yip! Ha ha ho ho and hee hee.

Arms swimming, feet firecrackering, he dances and dances.

When the song ends, the Chink puts the radio down as the news comes on.

> CHINK
> Personally, I prefer Stevie Wonder, but what the
> hell. Those cowgirls are always bitching because
> the only radio station in the area plays nothing but
> polkas, but I say you can dance to *anything* if you
> really feel like dancing.

The Chink dances a little to the news, and then lifts Sissy by her shoulders and guides her onto his pock-marked dance floor.

> SISSY
> But I don't know how to polka.

> CHINK
> Neither do I... ha ha ho ho hee hee.

The radio strikes up the "Lawrence Welk is a Hero of the Republic Polka," and the Chink and Sissy dance arm in arm, their shadows reel against the curves of the depression in the mountain.

Night birds fly past with fluttering feathers. A bat flies out of the cave.

The Chink escorts Sissy to a dark side of the depression and sits her down upon a pile of soft stuff: dried wheatgrass, faded Indian blankets and old down pillows without cases.

> SISSY
> (thinking)
> So this is how Jelly spends her visits to the Chink.

A twanging noise sounds from the bowels of the nearby cave.

> SISSY
> What was that?

> CHINK
> Clockworks.

> SISSY
> Clockworks?

The Chink pauses to decide whether he should talk any further, then proceeds.

                    CHINK
The Clockworks is one reason that I am here on
Siwash Ridge. I accepted the invitation to be
initiated as a shaman by an aged Siwash chief who was
the principle outside confederate of the Clock
People.

                    SISSY
Siwash, huh?

                    CHINK
He was a degenerated warlock who could turn
urine into beer, and the honor that he extended me
gave me rights of occupancy in this sacred cave on
this far-away Siwash Ridge. I came to the Dakota
hills to construct a clockworks of my own.

Sissy cradles her head in her arms, but is startled by a louder noise from
the clockworks. The Chink is startled too.

Bonk! sounds the cave, and then it chimes poing!

The Chink smiles at the noise coming from his clockworks.

                    CHINK
But unlike the clockworks of the Clock People, my
ticks more accurately echo the ticks of the
universe....(he listens)......ha ha ho ho and hee hee.

                    SISSY
The Clock People?

INT. CAVE NIGHT   (73)

The Chink leads Sissy into the cave where we see his clockworks. It is
made of garbage can lids and old saucepans and lard tins and car fenders
all wired together with baling wire. A bat flies into it making a *bong* noise
and the contraption moves a little.

CHINK
During the Second World War I busted out of Tule
Lake detention camp; as a Japanese-American, I
had been put there and watched over. I found
refuge with the Clock People, who discovered me in
a snow bank, near dead, I had been climbing
across the Sierra Nevada mountains.

SISSY
Then if you are Japanese, then why are you called
the Chink?

CHINK
The Clock People mistook me for Chinese. And the
name stuck. In the same way that all Indian
tribes came to be labeled "Indians" through the
ignorance of an Italian sailor with a taste for
oranges, it is only fitting that "Indians" misnamed
me. The Clock People, however, are not a tribe,
rather they are a gathering of Indians from various
tribes. They have lived together since 1906.

INT. THE GREAT BURROW   74

A gathering of the Clock People. A woman is giving birth near the Giant
timekeeping hourglass.

CHINK
The pivotal function of the Clock People is the
keeping and observing of the clockworks. It is a
real thing, and is kept at the center, at the soul, of
the Great Burrow. Insofar as it is possible, all Clock
People deaths and births occur in the presence of
the clockworks. Aside from birthing or dying, the
reason for the daily visits to the clockworks is to
check the time.

INT. SIWASH CAVE   NIGHT   75

Sissy listens to the Chink as they walk around the Chink's clockworks.

> CHINK
>
> These people have no other ritual than this one.
> Likewise, they have but one legend or cultural
> myth: that of a continuum they call the Eternity of
> Joy. It is into the Eternity of Joy that they believe
> all men will pass once the clockworks is destroyed.
> The destruction must come from the outside, must
> come by natural means, must come at the will of
> this gesticulating planet whose more acute stirrings
> thoughtless people call "earthquakes."

The Chink holds Sissy's thumbs in his hands adoringly.

> CHINK
>
> The Earth is alive. She burns inside with the heat
> of cosmic longing. She longs to be with her
> husband again. She moans. She turns softly in her
> sleep. In the Eternity of Joy, pluralized,
> deurbanized man, at ease with his gentle
> technologies, will smile and sigh when the Earth
> begins to shake. I loved those loony redskins, but I
> couldn't be a party to their utopian dreaming.
> After a while it occured to me that the Clock People
> waiting for the Eternity of Joy was virtually
> identical to the Christians waiting for the Second
> Coming. Or the Communists waiting for the
> worldwide revolution. Or the Debbies waiting for
> the flying saucers. All the same. Just more suckers
> betting their share of the present on the future,
> banking every misery on a happy ending to
> history. Well, history is ending every second -
> happily for some of us, unhappily for others,
> happily one second, unhappily the next. History is
> always ending and always not ending...ha ha ho ho
> and hee hee.

Sissy interrupts the Chink for a second while he is worshipping her thumbs.

                    SISSY
          What do you believe in then?

                    CHINK
          Ha ha ho ho and hee hee.

Then he says nothing. And his silence makes Sissy weep. They sit down on a grass floor, illuminated by the fire outside the cave.

Then the Chink, without hesitation, grasps her thumbs. He squeezes them, caresses them, covers them with wet kisses, telling them how beautiful they are.

Sissy is bowled over, frightened, stunned, elated, moved almost to tears.

Sissy bends her head back and whispers.

                    SISSY
          If this be adultery, make the most of it.

And as the Chink plunges into Sissy, she arches her spread bottom against the blankets and rears up to meet him halfway.

Their bodies glowing in the firelight, they cast shadows of ANCIENT BEINGS, anthropomorphs making love through the night under the moon.

INT. CAVE DAY   (76)

SUNBEAMS awaken Sissy. When she looks around she sees an inscription has been freshly scrawled on the right wall.

          I BELIEVE IN EVERYTHING; NOTHING IS SACRED.

And on the left wall:

I BELIEVE IN NOTHING; EVERYTHING IS SACRED.

Sissy hears and then sees A HELICOPTER in the sky above the ranch.
Sissy gets up and walks out of the cave.

EXT. TRAIL MORN   (77)

Sissy walks.

EXT. RUBBER ROSE   (78)

Sissy hitches a ride out of town.

EXT. FRONT DOORSTEPS   MORNING   (79)

Countless NEWSPAPERS on countless porches, and the headline of the St.
Louis *Post-Dispatch* reads:

OUR WHOOPING CRANES ARE MISSING.

INT. THE COUNTESS' OFFICE   DAY   (80)

The countess is in a snit.

> COUNTESS
> Sissy, don't play dumb with me! You're a good
> model but a shitty actress. The cowgirls are
> involved in this whooping crane disappearance.
> You know perfectly well they are. Last seen in
> Nebraska. Didn't make it to Canada. Siwash Lake is
> between Nebraska and Canada. The cowgirls have
> possession of Siwash Lake. And who else but
> Jellybean's wild cunts could possibly conceive of
> doing something so diabolical as to tamper with the
> last flock of some nearly extinct birds? How much
> do you know about it? Have they murdered those
> cranes the way they murdered my moo cows?

> SISSY
> I don't know anything about it.

> COUNTESS
> Sissy. You're trying to protect those scuzzy
> bitches. Well, let your conscience be your guide, as
> my mommy used to say, but it won't work. Those
> stinking sluts are going to suffer...

Sissy strikes the Countess with her right thumb - with astonishing force.

Immediately the thumb strikes again, this time shattering the Countess's
monocle against his eye.

> COUNTESS
> (gasping)
> Shit O dear.

HIS DENTURES fall onto the shag rug.

The *left* thumb strikes. Sissy is swinging her thumbs like ballbats socking
flaming homers over the left-field fence.

The countess is out on his feet. His eyes are closed. His legs wobble. He
does a pathetic dance, like a drunken old fool trying to boogie with a
chorus girl.

He topples forward and meets Sissy's onrushing thumb of thunder which
straightens him up, sends him over backward. Motionless, he lies on the
floor, a crimson part in his thinning hair, a bright ooze at each nostril.

INT. HOSPITAL DAY   (81)

Seated on a spotless wooden bench is Sissy, staring at a clock.
A surgeon emerges.

                    SURGEON
Well, he's not out of danger, but I think we can
safely say he's going to make it. I'd be pretty
surprised if he didn't. However, there is evidence
of injury to the frontal lobe, and I have reason to
fear that this injury may be permanent. The
patient may never again function as a normal
human being.

                    SISSY
Brain damage? You mean he's going to be a
vegetable?

                    SURGEON
Vegetable? Vegetable? I wouldn't say that, no.
We won't ascertain the extent of the injury for
some days. But there is a genuine possibility of
severe and lasting behavioral defects. I wouldn't
classify it in the vegetable category, however.

EXT. STREET DAY   (82)

SISSY IS HITCHING OUT OF TOWN

A conservative blue Econoline van out of the throngs of traffic draws itself
to Sissy as if on a string.

SISSY HOPS IN.

INT. VAN DAY   (83)

The DRIVER stomps on the gas. With a sense of disgust at her own failure
Sissy scrutinizes his sweaty brow, his smug hot leer, his starving eyes.

Her heart sinks when she sees his gun and his knife. He is also unzipping
his pants.

> DRIVER
>
> I'm going to give it to you like you've never had it
> before. Oh, you didn't know it could be this good.
> You're gonna like it. You're gonna like it. You're
> gonna like it so good. You're gonna love it so much
> you're gonna cry. You're gonna cry. You're gonna
> cry and cry. Do you like to cry? Do you like it
> when it hurts a little bit? Whatever happens to
> you, it'll be worth it. The way I'm gonna give it to
> you, it'll be worth anything. Everything. Go ahead
> and cry if you want to. I like it when women cry.
> It means they appreciate me.

EXT. STREET DAY

The van pulls over down a dead end alley between warehouses.

INT. VAN DAY

Sissy looks into the back at a soiled mattress.

The driver is taking his dick out of his pants. But with a swift swoosh,
Sissy's left thumb comes down hard on the penis top, making the driver
howl.

His finger fumbles for the gun trigger, but before he gets to it, Sissy's
thumb splats between his eyes. Twice. Three times. He loses control of
the van.

EXT. VAN DAY

It lumbers into a street lamp. Sissy leaps from the vehicle and runs.

INT. WORKING MAN'S LUNCHEONETTE DAY

Sissy goes in and begins to cry at the counter as she looks at her thumbs.

EXT. NEW JERSEY TURNPIKE DAY

Into a sunset hitches Sissy.

EXT. ROAD NIGHT   89

SISSY hops into a semi.

And Road signs: TRENTON   N.J.
                           BALTIMORE MD
                           WASHINGTON D.C.

            then   RICHMOND, VA

EXT. DR. DREYFUS'S HOUSE DAY   90

An older Dr. Dreyfus answers the door. Without Sissy's asking he speaks.

                    DR. DREYFUS
           I'm afraid I can't help you.

                    SISSY
           But Doctor.

                    DREYFUS
           Please, child, don't be dismayed. We all have
           problems these days. But as the painter Van Gogh
           said, 'Mysteries remain, sorrow or melancholy
           remains, but the everlasting negative is balanced
           by the positive work which thus is achieved, after
           all.' I don't suppose that means very much to you.
           I have retired.   A victim of a malpractice suit.

                    SISSY
                    (embracing him)
           Oh, Doctor! You've got to do it. You and nobody
           else should be allowed to take away my gift.

In her embrace, the Doctor is presented with her thumbs.

DR. DREYFUS
Ah, the thumb.

LATER sitting inside his study, Dreyfus muses.

DR. DREYFUS
The thumb the thumb the thumb the thumb the
thumb the thumb. One of evolution's most
ingenious inventions; a built-in tool sensitive to
texture, contour and temperature; an alchemical
lever; the secret key to technology; the link
between the mind and art; a humanizing device.
The marmoset and the lemur are thumbless; none
of the New World monkeys has opposable thumbs;
the spider monkey's thumbs are absent or reduced
to a tiny tubercle; the thumbs of the potto are set
at an angle of one hundred eighty degrees to the
other digits.

Pause.

DR. DREYFUS
And so you are demanding at last the privileges of
thumb that nature has perversely denied you?

SISSY
I just want to be normal, give me that old-
fashioned normality. It was good enough for Crazy
Horse and it's good enough for me.

DR. DREYFUS
Ah, yes. Very well, my dear. Here is what we can
do.

VIEWS OF   Sissy admitted to a hospital   91

Blood analyzed in a laboratory.

Powerful lamps turn on in an operating room.

IV tubes are inserted in veins.

Sissy is wheeled into surgery.

An anesthesiologist sticks a needle into a curved and creamy ass.

An anesthesiologist sticks needles into a long, graceful neck.

A nurse scrubs an arm.

A body and table are draped with sheets to create a sterile field.

A tourniquet is placed on a slender right arm.

An elastic rubber bandage is applied so tightly it squeezes most of the blood out of an arm.

A tourniquet is inflated.

A surgeon outlines in iodine an incision around the base of a thumb.

Pale smooth skin is incised along a premarked line and dissected down to the bone.

Woman flesh is sewn shut with four-ought nylon suture.

A tourniquet is deflated, a bloody arm bathed.

A young woman is rolled into a recovery room.

A nurse and two surgeons, their attention directed by an intensifying pinkish glow, turn to stare into a metal pan, where a huge human thumb, disarticulated from the hand it has been severed from, is now flopping about like a trout, or rather, arching and thrusting itself in a calculated and endlessly repeated gesture, the gesture of the hitchhike.

EXT. SKY DAY

Two representatives of the Fish and Wildlife Service are flying over Siwash Lake in a U.S. Forestry Service Helicopter.

THEY CAN SEE the whooping cranes by the side of the lake. And as they are recording this, shots from a band of young women on horseback drive them away.

EXT. RUBBER ROSE RANCH DAY

the same two agents are driving in a truck approaching the Rubber Rose Ranch. Two bullet ricochets spin off the hood and roof of their truck and they stop to see a lone teenaged cowgirl with a rifle.

EXT. RUBBER ROSE GATES DAY 94

An entourage of Forest Service Rangers, a county sheriff, four deputy shriffs, a state game warden and Mottburg's town marshall and several of *his* deputies, the editor of the Mottburg *Gazette* and a couple of bird watchers or two are met by...

AT LEAST FIFTEEN ARMED FEMALES at the gate of the Ranch. Through a bullhorn, Jelly speaks out at the entourage of law enforcement officers.

> JELLY
> Yep, the whooping cranes are here all right.
> They're in fine shape, and as you musta saw from
> your fucking whirly machine, unrestrained, free to
> go as they please. But this is private property and
> you aren't laying a foot on it. None of you.

                    SHERIFF
We'll be back with a court order and a fistful of
search warrants.

                    JELLY
Just come back with a couple of people who know
what they're doing and we'll let 'em in for a nice
close look at the birds.

                    DELORES
And make sure at least one of them is female, and
you better do as we say or there may be trouble.

AND OVER THE AIRWAVES an announcement is broadcast.

INT. WHITE HOUSE DAY   (95)

THE ASSISTANT INTERIOR UNDERSECRETARY IS SPEAKING INTO A
MICROPHONE FOR THE NEWS, and reading from a paper in his hand.

                    UNDERSECRETARY
It will be my extreme pleasure to report to the
President...

INT. SCHOOL AURITORIUM   (96)

Students listening...

                    UNDERSECRETARY
...who has been gravely concerned about the fate of
our whooping cranes....

EXT. CONSTRUCTION SITE DAY   (97)

Two construction workers high atop the city listening to a small transistor
radio and eating lunch.

>   UNDERSECRETARY
> ...and to the Interior Secretary and to the American
>   people that the entire flock of cranes is, indeed, at...

EXT. MALL DAY   (98)

A crowd of people listening to a broadcast in front of a bandstand set up in front of the mall.

>   UNDERSECRETARY VOICE
> ...Siwash Lake and in apparently healthy condition.

The crowd cheers.

>   UNDERSECRETARY VOICE
> ....The cranes have built brooding nests around the
>   whole circumference of the small lake, and have...

EXT. FIELD DAY   (99)

Cowgirls are watching a small television.

>   UNDERSECRETARY
> ....hatched chicks there. Counting the young birds,
>   there are now approximately sixty cranes in the
>   flock. While this is good news, it is also quite
>   bewildering...

EXT. RUBBER ROSE RANCH DAY   (100)

A vehicle know as "the peyote wagon" pulls out of the Rubber Rose. Delores del Ruby is at the wheel. And over her truck radio we hear:

>   UNDERSECRETARY V.O.
> ...Whooping cranes are territorily minded and have
>   never been known to nest as close as a mile to one
>   another, yet here they are virtually side by side.

EXT. HILL DAY   (101)

A lone FBI man sees the peyote wagon leaving the ranch through his binoculars.

INT. CAR NIGHT   (102)

Sissy hears a broadcast over a moving car radio.

>   NEWS REPORTER
>   The Rubber Rose Ranch has issued a communiqué
>   that was sent to the federal judge and copies of a
>   recording to the press, today.

We can hear the voice of Bonanza Jellybean:

>   BONANZA JELLYBEAN
>   (over the radio)
>   THE WHOOPING CRANE HAS BEEN DRIVEN TO THE
>   EDGE OF EXTINCTION BY AN AGGRESSIVE, BRUTAL
>   PATERNALISTIC SYSTEM INTENT ON SUBDUING
>   THE EARTH AND ESTABLISHING ITS DOMINION
>   OVER ALL THINGS - IN THE NAME OF GOD THE
>   FATHER, LAW, ORDER AND ECONOMIC PROGRESS.

Sissy recognizes the voice.

>   SISSY
>   That's Jellybean!

>   JELLY V.O.
>   FROM MEN, THE WHOOPING CRANE HAS RECEIVED
>   NEITHER LOVE NOR RESPECT. MEN HAVE DRAINED
>   THE CRANE'S MARSHES, STOLEN ITS EGGS, INVADED
>   ITS PRIVACY, POLLUTED ITS FOOD, FOULED ITS
>   AIR, BLOWN IT APART WITH BUCKSHOT.

INT. RANCH OFFICE,   (103)

Jelly is on the telephone.

> JELLY
> OBVIOUSLY, A PATERNALISTIC SOCIETY DOES NOT
> DESERVE ANYTHING AS GRAND AND BEAUTIFUL
> AND WILD AND FREE AS THE WHOOPING CRANE.
> YOU MEN HAVE FAILED IN YOUR DUTY TO THE
> CRANE. NOW IT IS WOMEN'S TURN. THE CRANES
> ARE IN OUR CHARGE NOW. WE WILL PROTECT
> THEM AS LONG AS THEY STILL REQUIRE
> PROTECTION -

INT. HOSPITAL RECOVERY ROOM DAY   (104)

Sissy listens to the radio.

> JELLY'S VOICE
> WHILE WORKING TOWARD A DAY WHEN THE
> CREATURES OF THE WORLD NO LONGER HAVE TO
> SUFFER MAN'S EGOISM, INSENSITIVITY AND GREED.
> WE REFUSE YOUR ORDER. WE SAY TAKE YOUR
> ORDER AND SHOVE IT. THIS FLOCK OF BIRDS IS
> STAYING WITH US. GET LOST, MAC.

EXT. ROAD DAY   (105)

Sissy is hitchhiking with her new thumb. But cars pass one after another
without stopping. Until Sissy finally tries her *left* thumb, which has been
spared the knife.

With this thumb there are new maneuvers to try out.   And as soon as she
does, a car stops.

MOSAIC of hitchiking brilliance with Sissy's use of her left thumb. A
CLOCK IS TICKING past twelve then on to six and past eight.... she
dances wildly around traffic, stopping the hardest of drivers, THE
CLOCK TICKS AWAY and within thirty hours she is approaching
Mottburg again.

EXT. RUBBER ROSE DAY   (106)

The Ranch is now surrounded by two hundred federal marshalls reinforced
by a dozen FBI agents with loaded guns taking position outside
the ranch.

Sissy gets out of her car and walks past the posse and through the gates.

Kym carries a radio which is playing "The Day-Old Apple Strudel Polka"
across the corral. She carries the radio as if it is a suitcase full of skunk
lice.

> KYM
> Man, this is the stupidest music I've ever heard.
> This radio should have stayed in the privy where it
> belongs.

Kym ropes the radio to her saddle horn and prepares to give it a ride
across the Dakota hills. She gets on her horse and rides by the Ranch
bungalows and spies Sissy sitting in the outhouse.

> SISSY
Howdy.

Kym gets off her horse and hugs Sissy.

> KYM
> You know what you're getting into if you come over
> to the lake...

> SISSY
> Yes, but I want to be there. I want to see
> Jellybean. I want to see the cranes.

(107)

THEY RIDE ACROSS THE HILLS. Then they stop at an outlook and Sissy
sees the circular barricade in the field below.

> KYM
> We heard on the radio that the judge has set
> Delores's bail at fifty thousand dollars. Now she
> won't be here when we really need her.

EXT. CAMP DAY ⟨108⟩

A few cowgirls in the camp huddle around a radio:

> RADIO NEWS REPORT
> The American Civil Liberties Union has requested
> an extension for the Rubber Rose Ranch. The
> government is aware of the inflamed situation and
> are afraid that all the marshals and agents might
> be too willing to uncork the bottle of blood...

SISSY RIDES INTO CAMP on the back of Kym's horse the way that John
Wayne would have ridden into the Alamo; Heather, Bonanza Jellybean,
Debbie, Elaine and Linda dance up to meet her.

Before Sissy is completely on the ground, Jelly's tongue is in her mouth.
She stumbles out of a stirrup into a wiggly embrace.

> JELLY
> Let's celebrate!

Debbie stokes up a big joint right now, as Jelly gets out her six guns and
fires them in the air. Heather twirls and jumps through her rope.

The "Unsung Hero Returns Polka" strikes up on the radio.

Elaine rears up on her horse.

EXT. HILLSIDE DAY ⟨109⟩

FROM AFAR, AN FBI AGENT views the little going on.

> AGENT
> Ain't that just like women.

But as the Agent is saying this, viewing them from the ridge, a large rock tumbles down the hill and grazes his head, knocking him out.

VIEW of the side of the ridge from where the rock came, but there is strangely nothing where we expect to see the Chink.

BELOW: The cowgirls.   (110)

> JELLY
> Looks like every time we get together things are in
> a mess.

> SISSY
> So be it.   It looks serious this time, though. All
> these guns...are you actually prepared to kill and
> die for whooping cranes?

> JELLY
> Hell no, the cranes are wonderful, okay, but I'm not in
> this for whooping cranes. I'm in it for cowgirls. If we
> cowgirls give in to authority on this crane issue, then
> cowgirls become just another compromise. I want a finer
> fate than that - for me and for every other cowgirl.
> Better no cowgirls at all than cowgirls compromised.

> SISSY
> How did this business get started, anyhow? Why
> are the birds nesting here?

> DEBBIE
> You were aware that we were feeding them, weren't you?
> We fed them brown rice and they stayed over a couple of
> extra days. Then we decided to try something different.
> We mixed our brown rice with fishmeal - whoopers love
> seafood, and fishmeal is cheap. Then Delores suggested
> another ingredient, and we think that's what did the trick.

SISSY

You mean...

DEBBIE AND JELLY TOGETHER

PEYOTE!

SISSY

They're drugged.

JELLY

Aw, come off it, Sissy. What do you mean,
'drugged'? Every living thing is a chemical
composition and anything that is added to it
changes that composition. When you eat a
cheeseburger or a Three Musketeers bar, it changes
your body chemistry. The kind of food you eat, the
kind of air you breathe, can change your mental
state. Does that mean you're 'drugged'?

Sissy frames the flock with the hole in the center of her cheese sandwich.

SISSY

No, I guess not.

JELLY

'Drugged' is a stupid word.

SISSY

But the peyote is obviously affecting their brains.
It's made them break a migratory pattern that goes
back thousands of years.

DEBBIE

The way I see it, is that the peyote mellowed them
out. Made them less uptight. They were afraid of
bad weather and humans. That's why they
migrated and kept to themselves. But the peyote
has enlightened them. It's taught them there is
nothing to fear but fear itself. Now they're digging

life and letting the bad vibes slide on. Don't worry,
be happy. Be here now.

> SISSY
> Fear in wild animals is completely different from
> paranoia in people. In the wilderness ecosystem,
> fear is natural and necessary. It's merely a
> mechanism for maintaining life. If the cranes
> hadn't had a capacity for fear, they would have
> disappeared long ago and you'd be having to get
> loaded with common old everyday meadowlarks
> and mallards.

> JELLY
> This here discussion is destined to become
> academic. Because we've got less than half a bag of
> peyote buttons left and Delores's run ended up in
> the Mottburg jail. So any day now we'll get a
> chance to see how the whoopers behave when they
> come down, to see if the peyote experience really
> changed them or not. But in the meantime, I want
> to say this about fear.....

Then Sissy and Jelly hear a news broadcast on the radio.

> ANNOUNCER
> Judge Greenfield, at the request of the ACLU, has
> granted a forty-eight-hour extension of the
> deadline by which the Rubber Rose cowgirls must comply
> with his order. Negotiations between the cowgirls
> and the government are expected to follow.
> Another item in, the forewoman of the Rubber Rose
> Ranch, a Delores del Ruby is now free on bond after
> having been arrested in Mottburg with more than
> fifty pounds of peyote buttons. Her bail has been
> paid by the owner of the besieged ranch, Countess
> Products, Inc. Miss del Ruby's bail having come
> from the tycoon's personal advisor, a certain Dr.
> Robbins of New York City.

                    SISSY
          Dr. Robbins?

EXT. PRAIRIE NIGHT   (111)

Sissy and Jelly lie under the same stars, under the same blankets. Under
the same spell.

                    JELLY
          Every time I tell you that I love you, you flinch.
          But that's *your* problem.

                    SISSY
          If I flinch when you say you love me, it's both our
          problems. My confusion becomes your confusion.
          Students confuse teachers, patients confuse
          psychiatrists, lovers with confused hearts confuse
          lovers with clear hearts....

EXT. CAMPFIRE NIGHT   (112)

Delores and some of the other cowgirls are talking.   A sharp wind is
beginning to gust.
                    DELORES
          It isn't for ourselves that we take this stand. It
          isn't for cowgirls. It's for all the daughters
          everywhere. This is an extremely important
          confrontation. This is womankind's chance to prove
          to her enemy that she's willing to fight and die. If
          we women don't show here and now that we aren't
          afraid to fight and die, then our enemy will never
          take us seriously. Men will always know that, no
          matter how strong our words and determined our
          deeds, there's a point where we'll back down and
          give them their way.

Delores cracks her whip then parades around the campfire.

> DELORES
> I'm prepared to win! Victory for every female,
> living or dead, who's suffered the temporary
> defeats of masculine insensitivity to their inner
> lives!

A few of the cowgirls cheer.

> DONNA
> I'll fight the bastards.

Big Red opens a can of beans with a Bowie knife.

> BIG RED
> I'll fight 'em with bean gas, if necessary.

Delores snaps her whip again.

> DELORES
> The sun's going down. Let's those of us not
> standing watch get some sleep. In the morning
> we'll plan our fight. Tomorrow afternoon those of
> you who'd like can join me in the reeds, where the
> cranes and I will be sharing the last crumbs left in
> the peyote sack.

EXT. SIWASH LAKE DAY   (113)

Delores del Ruby appears from the reeds at Siwash Lake's
edge, asleep yet awake. She has sunk so deep into the hole in her mind
that gale and dust could not follow her.

AS SHE APPROACHES THE COWGIRL CAMP, THEY GATHER AROUND HER IN
A TIGHT CIRCLE.

MANY ARE TRANSFIXED as they listen.

DELORES

It is woman's mission to destroy as well as to give
birth. We will destroy the tyranny of the dull. But
we can't destroy it with guns. Or whips. Violence
is the dullard's Breakfast of Champions and the
logical end product of his or her misplaced pride.
Violence fertilizes that which we would starve.

No, we will destroy the enemy in other ways. The
Peyote Mother has promised a Fourth Vision. But it
won't come to me alone. It will come to each of
you, to every cowgirl in the land, when you have
overcome that in your own self which is dull.

The Fourth Vision will come to some men too. You
will recogize them when you meet them, and be
their steady sidekicks in equal and ecstatic
escapades of poetic behavior and romance.

Delores holds up a card. The prairie moon illuminates its tattered edges. It
is the jack of hearts.

The forewoman seems to be tiring. Fumes of weariness stream from her
black hair. Her voice is leaning against the wall of her larynx when she
says:

DELORES

First thing, you must end this business with the
government and the cranes. It's been positive and
fruitful, but it's gone far enough. Playfulness
ceases to serve a serious purpose when it takes
itself too seriously. Sorry I won't be with you at
the conclusion. As you know, I've been sick and
stupid   for a long time. I have a lot to make up
for, a lot to accomplish, and there's someone
important that I've got to see. Now.

As graceful as a ballet for cobras, Delores turns and walks away into the
night.

EXT. RANCH GATES   DAY

THE FBI, other VIGILANTES and POLICEMEN wait in anticipation of an attack outside of the boundaries of the ranch.

EXT. THE COWGIRL COMPOUND   DAY

Jelly is addressing the group of cowgirls.

> JELLY
> Well, what we got to do is one of us has got to go up that hill and tell them boys that America can have its whooping cranes back. Since I'm the boss here, and since I'm responsible for a lot of you choosing to be cowgirls in the first place, it's gonna be me that goes...

Small protests from the circle of cowgirls.

> JELLY
> No buts about it. It's getting lighter by the second. You podners keep your heads down . Ta ta.

The cutest cowgirl in the world stood up and stretched out.

> COWGIRL
> Jelly! Please!

But Jelly is already on her way.

BONANZA JELLYBEAN VAULTS over the carcass of a reducing machine and plants her Tony Lama boots in the stirrup of her saddle and straddles her horse and takes off.

EXT. COMPOUND DAY

The posse surrounding the ranch, can see Jelly coming over the hill on her horse at a full gallop.

EXT. HILL DAY (117)

Jelly stops her horse, looks down at her waist, and sees her sixguns.

> JELLY
> Better get rid of these. Might give those greenhorn
> dudes a fright.

THROUGH the scope of an FBI rifle, Jelly is drawing her gun out of her
holster.

> AGENT
> She's going to fire....

He squeezes the trigger, and Jelly is caught in the stomach with a bullet.
She falls off her horse to the ground.

(118)

THE CHINK sees Bonanza Jellybean cut down from a vantage point on the
hill, and makes a beeline for the government barricades, SHOUTING.

(119)

THE COWGIRLS scream and cry, and grab their weapons. A couple of them
leap from the barricade and are immediately riddled.

EXT. HILL morn (120)

The six-gun slips from her fingers.

Twenty or thirty more sweaty triggers are squeezed on the hilltop firing at
Bonanza Jellybean.

THE CHINK RUNNING AND SHOUTING. (121)

EXT. COWGIRL CAMP DAY

A VOICE OVER THE BULLHORN directed at the cowgirls echos:

> VOICE
> You've got two minutes to come out with you hands
> over your heads!

RANDOM G-MEN are sniping at the cowgirls, making it impossible to
surrender.

A stray bullet SENDS THE CHINK back down the hillside, beard, robe and
sandals flying.

IN THE HUSH that follows, in the echos of the explosive fire, the whooping
crane flock rises in one grand assault of beating feathers - a lily white
storm of life, a gush of albino Gabriels - swarm into the waiting sky, and
circle the pond one time before flapping south toward Texas...

...they cast shadows over a dead Jellybean who is literally biting the dust.

Sissy lifts Jelly out of the dust and holds her. Sissy lifts Jelly's
satin shirt tail and pulls down the waistband of her skirt. Bright red blood
is running out of her scar.

> JELLY
> Right in the scar where I fell on a wooden horse
> when I was twelve. Haw, I wasn't *really* shot with
> a silver bullet.

Confessing to Sissy.

> JELLY
> Or was I?

EXT. NEW YORK SKY

The cranes fly over the Statue of Liberty.

EXT. PARISIAN SKY (124)

The Cranes fly over the Eiffel tower.

EXT. RUSSIAN SKY (125)

The Cranes fly over Red Square.

INT. MORGUE DAY (126)

An undertaker pounding five nails into a white coffin. ON THE TOP OF THE COFFIN are engraved two crossed GOLD SIXGUNS. There are eleven famous cowgirls enameled on the edges and in the middle it reads:

BONANZA JELLYBEAN
1944-1973
"Ha ha ho ho and hee hee"

title card: (127)

The brown paper bag

A brown paper bag is sitting on the side of the road.

> A VOICE
> The brown paper bag is the only thing civilized
> man has produced that does not seem out of place
> in nature. Crumpled into a wad of wrinkles, like the
> fossilized brain of a dryad; its kinship to tree (to
> knot and nest) unobscured by the cruel crush of
> industry; absorbing the elements like any other
> organic entity; blending with rock and vegetation as
> if it were a burrowing owl's doormat or a jack
> rabbit's underwear, a No. 8 Kraft paper bag lay
> discarded in the hills of Dakota and appeared to
> live where it lay. Once long ago, it had borne a

package of buns and a jar of mustard to a
kitchenette rendezvous with a fried hamburger.
More recently, the bag had held ....love letters.

View of a bunkhouse trunk.   (128)

> VOICE
> As a hole in an oak hides a squirrel's family
> jewels, the bag had hidden love letters in
> the bottom of a bunkhouse trunk.

Hands lift the contents of the trunk away, rope, spurs, and blanket and
find the hidden sack of letters.

> VOICE
> Then one day after work, the button-nosed
> little cowgirl to whom the letters were
> addressed gathered bag and contents under her
> arm, slipped out to the corral...

We see the Cowgirl saddling her horse late in the day.   (129)

> VOICE
> ...past ranch hands pitching horseshoes and
> ranch hands flying Tibetan kites, saddled up
> and trotted into the hills.

We see the Cowgirl riding along a ridge.   (130)

> VOICE
> A mile or so from the bunkhouse, she dismounted
> and built a small fire; she fed the fire letters.

                                                               (131)

And this we see also, the lonely Cowgirl feeding the letters to a fire in the
dusky early night. We can see the cowgirl is Sissy Hankshaw.

> VOICE
> ...one by one, the way her girl friend had
> once fed her french fries.

She is crying now and feeding the fire, close of words like "always" and "forever" burning up.

> VOICE
> As words such as "sweethheart" and "honey
> britches" and "forever" and "always" burned away,
> the cowgirl squirted a few tears. Her eyes were so
> misty she forgot to burn the bag.

INT. BUNKHOUSE NIGHT.   (132)

Sissy is sobbing.

Big Red offers a piece of homemade fudge and shows no surprise when Sissy refuses it.

Kym kisses the lips quickly of the despondent Cowgirl, and the bunkhouse lights go out.

Delores plunks a carefree song on an old Gibson, looks up at the moon.

> DELORES
> You know, podner, you can tune a guitar but
> you can't tuna fish.

She plunks a few notes.

> DELORES
> God, but it's good to be a cowgirl.

And the bunkhouse lights are turned off. There are some giggles from the cowgirls.

INT. MAIN BEDROOM   RANCH   DAY   (133)

THE CHINK wakes up and is being cared for by Sissy. He is in pain, but
winking.

> SISSY
> Is everything getting worse?

> CHINK
> Yes, everything *is* getting worse. But everything is
> also getting better.

> SISSY
> The Countess has come to our aid. The Rubber
> Rose Ranch is officially deeded to all the cowgirls.
> And I have been asked to oversee the ranch. For
> $300 a week.   And as it turns out, the Countess is
> not going to be the vegetable the doctors thought
> he was...here's a picture!

Sissy shows a picture of the Countess recovering in a hospital bed, posing
next to Doctor Robbins.

> CHINK
> I want to go back to the Clock People. I kind of
> miss those fool redskins and wonder what they're
> up to. What's happened to Jelly?

> SISSY
> She had a one way-ticket to Kansas City.

> CHINK
> You mean she's dead?

The Chink mourns a bit.

> SISSY
> But that's an old story now...... I can't believe that
> you would leave the Butte.

CHINK

Easy come, easy go.

DELORES

Wow, you sure have a way with words.

The Chink looks over and sees that Delores is standing in the doorway.

CHINK

I can't help it if I grew up in an antipoetic culture. Language will be different when I'm with the Clock People though. They're from an oral tradition. And I'm not talking about what you horny hop toads do in bed every night.

The Chink smiles.

Delores blushes.

SISSY

Well, if the Clock People give you any inside information on the end of the world, drop us a postcard.

CHINK

The world isn't going to end, you dummy; I hope you know that much. (He grows uncharacteristically serious.) But it *is* going to change. It's going to change drastically, and probably in your lifetime. The Clock People see calamitous earthquakes as the agent of change, and they may be right, since there are a hundred thousand earthquakes a year and major ones are long overdue. But there are far worse catastrophes coming... unless the human race can bring itself to abandon the goals and values of civilization, in other words, unless it can break the consumption habit - and we are so conditioned to consuming as a way of life that for most of us life would have no meaning without the yearnings and rewards of progressive consumption. It isn't merely that our bad habits will *cause* global catastrophes, but that our operative political-economic philosophies have us in such a blind crab grip that they prevent us from preparing for the natural disasters that are not our fault. So the apocalyptic shit is going to hit the fan, all right, but there'll be some of us it'll miss. Little pockets of humanity. Like the Clock People. Like you two honeys, if you decide to accept my offer of a lease on Siwash Cave. There's almost no worldwide calamity - famine, nuclear accident, plague, weather warfare or reduction of the ozone shield - that you couldn't survive in that cave.

He begins to caress Sissy's belly. His eyes are smiling. Sissy is surprised.

CHINK

Suppose that you bear five or six children with your characteristics. All in Siwash Cave. In a postcatastrophe world, your offspring would of necessity intermarry, forming in time a tribe. A tribe every member of which had giant thumbs. A tribe of Big Thumbs would relate to the environment in very special ways. It could not use weapons or produce sophisticated tools. It would have to rely on its wits and its senses. It would have to live with animals - and plants! - as virtual equals. It's extremely pleasant to me to think about a tribe of physical eccentrics living peacefully with animals and plants, learning their languages, perhaps, and paying them the respect they deserve.

SISSY

How am I going to be the progenitor of a tribe when I'm living on an isolated ridgetop with Delores?

> CHINK
> That's your problem.

The Chink coughs.

> CHINK
> Listen to the way I'm babbling. That bullet must
> have loosened one of my transistors. Don't pay any
> attention to me. You've got to work it out for
> yourself. The westbound choo-choo leaves
> Mottburg at one-forty. I want to be on it. Will you
> drive me to the station?

INT. TRUCK DAY (134)

Sissy and Delores are driving the Chink out the front gate of the Rubber
Rose.

> CHINK
> Schedules! Ironic how I have to follow timetables
> in order to get back to the clockworks.

He yells out the window of the moving vehicle.

> CHINK
> Don't ever bet against paradox, ladies...

EXT. THE RUBBER ROSE GATES (135)

We hear the Chink yelling, and the Rubber Rose sign is being changed to
one that reads **El Rancho Jellybean**.

> CHINK
> ....if complexity doesn't beat you, then paradox will.
> Ha ha ho ho and hee hee.....

And the truck disappears into the prairie land.

(136)

A LONG DARK PAUSE, UNTIL finally we are inside the cave where the Chink's Clockworks are at work..................................*poing!*

It is revealed that Sissy is with Delores snug in the old hermit's living quarters. She listens to the clinking of the Chink's Clockworks.

And feels her belly.

The swell of her belly has forced her to sleep on her back.

CLOSE VIEW of Sissy's belly, and a little foot kicks from inside. Or is it a foot?

(137)

VIEW INSIDE THE BELLY of Sissy's unborn baby. It is half-Japanese, one thirty-second Siwash and all thumbs.

The moving thumbs are hitchhiking *you* .....

The end.

m y   o W N

P R I v a T e

i d A H o

a screenplay   by   Gus Van Sant

revised Apr. '89

My Own Private Idaho was first shown at the Venice Film Festival in 1991. The cast includes:

MIKE WATERS	River Phoenix
SCOTT FAVOR	Keanu Reeves
RICHARD WATERS	James Russo
BOB PIGEON	William Reichert
GARY	Rodney Harvey
CARMELLA	Chiara Caselli
DIGGER	Michael Parker
DENISE	Jessie Thomas
BUDD	Flea
ALENA	Grace Zabriskie
JACK FAVOR	Tom Troupe
HANS	Udo Kier
JANE LIGHTWORK	Sally Curtice
WALT	Robert Lee Pitchlynn
DADDY CARROLL	Mickey Cottrell
WADE	Wade Evans

Directors of Photography	Eric Alan Edwards
	John Campbell
Editor	Curtiss Clayton
Production Designer	David Brisbin
Costume Designer	Beatrix Aruna Pasztor
Music	Bill Stafford
Executive Producer	Gus Van Sant
Co-executive Producer	Allan Mindel
Producer	Laurie Parker
Screenplay	Gus Van Sant
	Additional dialogue by
	William Shakespeare
Director	Gus Van Sant

Produced by New Line Cinema

Views OF THE CITY OF Portland Oregon *digressing into
the seedy areas of the small city.*
*ARCADES, and yellow storefronts, of PORNOGRAPHIC
BOOKSHOPS.*

*A FEW YOUNG MEN LOITER IN FRONT OF ONE OF THE
BOOKSHOPS SOLICITOUSLY AND EYE A CUSTOMER.*

WHO ENTERS THE BOOKSHOP.

INSIDE, WE SEE:
Counters displaying COLORFUL COMIC-LIKE plastic covered
MAGAZINE and BOOK COVERS with names like HONCHO
– BUTCH – JOYBOY. INDICATING A Homo-erotic section
of the bookshop.

GROUPS OF MEN loiter about the magazine shop flipping
through the books and disappearing in and out of
curtained doors.

THE COUNTERMAN is on the phone.

Next to him is a particularly interesting YOUNG MAN on
the cover of one of the magazines – a bright yellow
background, jeans open two buttons on the top,
shirtless wearing a black cowboy hat. This character is
named SCOTT.

FULL VIEW of the MAGAZINE cover as Scott comes to life
– and talks to us.

                    SCOTT
          *I never thought I could be a real model, you know
          fashion-shit, cause I'm better at full body stuff.
          It's okay so long as the photographer doesn't come
          on to you and expect something for no pay. I'm
          trying to make a living, you know, and I like to be
          professional. 'Course if the guy wants to pay me,*

SCOTT (continued)
then shit/yeah. Here I am for him. I'll sell my
ass, I do it on the street all the time for cash.
And I'll be on the cover of a book. It's when you
start doing it for free that you start to grow wings,
Right, Mike?

ACROSS THE AISLE ON ANOTHER SHELF IS ANOTHER
COVER OF A MAGAZINE, AND ANOTHER YOUNG MAN ON
THE COVER STARTS TO MOVE AND SPEAK, ADDRESSING
SCOTT.

This character is named MIKE. (MIKE SHOULD BE
DIFFERENT FROM SCOTT, MIKE SHOULD BE BLOND AND
SCOTT SHOULD BE BROWN HAIRED, ALTHOUGH BOTH
POSSESS A CERTAIN PAINFUL DOWN AND OUT
HANDSOMENESS OF A STREET HUSTLER.)

MIKE
What are you talking about.   What wings?

SCOTT
Wings, man, you grow wings and become a
FAIRY.

MIKE
I ain't no fairy.

ANOTHER COVERBOY INTERRUPTS MIKE AND SCOTT'S
DISCUSSION, BUTTING IN.

COVERBOY
He ain't saying you is a fairy, faggot, he's
saying that if you go working for free then you
has no choice, you turn into a fairy, with
wings and all. That's all he mean, dunk.

MIKE (to Scottie)
Well, nevertheless, what do you care about
doing stuff for free or for money, shit. You're
going to inherit a bunch of money, you might
as well do it for free.

>   COVERBOY
>   *Is that right, sweetie?*

OTHER COVERBOYS PERK UP AND START FLIRTING WITH
SCOTT.

>   COVERBOY 2
>   *How much is a bunch of money, honey?*

>   COVERBOY 3
>   *What are you doing on the cover of that
>   magazine, slumming?*

Scott listens to all of them then looks back at Mike.

Mike smiles.

>   SCOTT
>   (to us)
>   *Actually, I'm on the street to settle a bet with
>   my goddamned stone-faced old man. I've
>   decided to live away from home for three
>   years. To prove a point. That I can live on
>   my own. And to appreciate the value of a
>   dollar. And Mike is right, there, I am going to
>   inherit money. A lot of money.*

I d A h o

The desert in the daytime.
MIKE enters the frame in front of a blue sky filled with
white clouds. He has a Texaco gas station attendant's
shirt on with a name tag that reads: BILL (not Mike,
his name).

The clouds are puffy against a deep blue sky. The road
is red. Purple mountains surround Mike on all sides far
in the distance, ten miles away. Mike looks in front of
him at a long stretch of road that disappears into the
horizon.

Mike looks at his wristwatch on his arm. He times how
long it takes to walk ten steps down the road.
Ten seconds. He glances back at a duffle bag. The duffle
bag falls over.

Mike looks at the picturesque sights surrounding him.
A wind sends a tumbleweed into the air. He takes ten
steps back to his duffle bag and checks watch again.

The sun is now setting.

                    MIKE
            (to himself)
        You can always tell where you are by the way
        the road looks. Like I just know that I been to
        this place before. I just know that I been
        stuck here like this one fuckin' time before,
        you know that?

ON THE SIDE OF THE ROAD A JACKRABBIT IS LISTENING
TO HIM.

                    MIKE
          There ain't no other road on earth that looks
          like this road. I mean, exactly like this road.
          (sniffs)
          One of a kind. (Sniffs) Like someone's face.
          Like a fucked up face...

THE ROAD HAS A DEFINITE FACE. TWO DISTANT CACTUS
FOR EYES – A CLOUD SHADOW FOR A MOUTH, MOUNTAINS
FOR HAIR.

                    MIKE
          Once you see it, even for a second, you
          remember it, and you better not forget it, you
          gotta remember people and who they are,
          right? Friends and enemies. You gotta
          remember the road and where it is too...

MIKE SUDDENLY LUNGES AT THE LITTLE RABBIT
LISTENING TO HIS CHAT ON THE SIDE OF THE ROAD, AND
THE RABBIT RUNS FOR HIS LIFE.

                    MIKE
          I just love to scare things...I don't know. It
          gives me a sense of....Power.

Mike thinks about the loneliness of the road.

                    MIKE
          This is nowhere. I'll bet that nobody is ever
          going to drive down this road. I'll be stuck
          here forever.

Mike looks at the road stressfully. The road looks back.
He looks at the road.....his eyes growing heavy. The
road looks back...

Mikes yawns.

                    MIKE'S VOICE OVER
          I don't know when it was I recognized I had
this disease.

Mike looks like a backwoods character who fits into the
terrain. Mike makes strange movements, like he is
having a sort of epileptic fit, then yawns like he is very
tired, again.

> MIKE'S VOICE OVER
> Sometimes I'll be in one place, and I'll close my
> eyes...

MIKE CLOSES HIS EYES. THEN A WHOLE RITUAL OF
EVENTS HAPPENS, HIS EYES TURN BACK IN HIS HEAD
AND HE BEGINS TO SHAKE ALL OVER. THEN ALL GOES
BLACK.

> MIKE'S VOICE OVER
> When I open them again, I'll be in a
> completely different surrounding.

When Mike opens his eyes, he is in downtown
PORTLAND, OREGON.

A LOUD BUS drives by Mike's view in the city. He is
asleep, then wakes enough to see other UNKNOWN KIDS
rifling his pockets in a doorway, as Mike sleepily looks
on.

> SUBTITLES
> It's kind of like time travel. It's kind of good.

MIKE CLOSES HIS EYES AGAIN, AND WHEN HE OPENS
THEM HE IS BACK IN THE COUNTRY. BUT THIS TIME A
COMPLETELY DIFFERENT TERRAIN. LIKE A LONG TIME
HAS PASSED. HE IS ALSO WEARING DIFFERENT CLOTHES.

MIKE CHECKS HIS WATCH AGAIN. He looks happy at the
passage of time.

> MIKE
> Yeah. It's kind of good. Passes the time.
> Unwanted as it is.

MIKE LEANS AGAINST THE DUFFLE BAG WITH HIM.   HE
LOOKS INTO THE FIELD next to him.   The wind blows a
paper cup into the air.

Mike watches the cup tumble in the air, and with a few
notes, a GUITAR follows. Then an uprooted cactus.

The paper cup, cactus and guitar lyrically trade places
in the air, and are followed by a large barn, which
twists and turns, then crashes directly into the middle
of the road.

On the road.   Riding in the back of a pickup truck.
Mike's shirt ruffles wildly in the wind, traveling at 60
mph.

And the truck disappears into the sun, toward a steep
mountain range.

L A *s   v e G A s*

O

*M*ike is walking down a LONELY ALLEYWAY in the
city. ALL OF A SUDDEN he is surrounded by three
BLACK BOYS, who are smiling and joking.

> BLACK 1
> SAY, WHITE BOY, where you goin'?

Black 1 pulls out a knife and waves it at Mike.

> BLACK 1
> What's in the sack. Let's see.

Mike fights with the guy for his sack. The Black cuts
Mike's hands with his knife but Mike won't let go.

In terror he watches his hands get cut, but he won't let
go. Mike starts to yawns and does the jitters to the
Black's amazement and drops to the ground. Scottie,
the older boy on the magazine cover, comes to Mike's
aid. He pushes the Black boy over, throws some trash
cans in their direction.

> BLACK 1
> This gonna be fun. Come on...

Scottie keeps fighting them off.

> SCOTTIE
> Man, what do you want from us, we haven't
> got anything.

The Blacks chuckle. Then they stop and slowly walk
away from Scott who hovers protectively around Mike's
body on the ground.

                    BLACK   (o.s.)
        Faggot!

We are in the city of Las Vegas in the daytime. (We are
aware of this because one character, RAY, is reading
the Las Vegas Chronicle.) —Mike sleeps, as a shopkeeper
washes his windows and three other street kids, Gary,
Ray and Scottie, are hanging around on the corner with
him.

Gary is hitting a public wastebasket with the end of a
stick as a MAN in a MERCEDES BENZ drives by them
very slowly, and looks at each one of the boys
individually. Gary pauses for a moment and poses.

                    RAY
            (to the man in the car)
        What's up?

                        MAN   (in German)
            [*Entschuldiging, junge...*]

The man in the car speeds off.

INT. CAR DAY.

THE MAN has the look of Rainer Fassbinder and Geraldo
Rivera as the same man; is of average build and has a
wash of hair gracing his forehead that looks quite
foreign. He turns to the right three times, as he is
circling his car.

OUT THE WINDOW OF THE CAR, we see the boys again.

EXT. STREET
                    GARY
        What's this guy want, think he wants to
        party?

                    SCOTT
He said "Entschuldiging, junge."

                    GARY
What's that mean? "Suck my dick?" Does he
want to suck my dick?

                    SCOTT
It means, "Excuse me, boys."

                    GARY
How the fuck do you know.

                    SCOTT
I've studied German, in prep school.

                    GARY
You know, Scottie, I don't know when to
believe you.

                    SCOTT
Here he comes again.

THE MAN leans out the window of his car.

                    MAN
        HELLO?

Gary leans into the man's car.

                    GARY
        Hey, dude.

                    MAN
        (speaks with a thick German accent)
        Excuse me. Can I speak to the young man over
        there, with the blond hair, ya?

                    GARY
        Who, that kid there? You can't talk with him
        now, he's asleep.

> MAN
> Can you wake him up?

> GARY
> No, you can't wake him...he's....but, what
> about me? Don't you want to talk with me?

The man is not interested in talking to Gary.

He shakes his head no, bothered by Gary.

> SCOTT
> (speaking fluent German)
> *Was willst du in Gottesname mit uns Juenge?*
> *Mach' es klar oder fahre ab!*
> (What in the hell do you want with us
> young kids, be specific or get out.)

> MAN
> (surprised)
> *Du bisst sehr intelligent mit deinem Aksent...*
> *Fuer einen Puppejunge.*
> (You are very clever with an accent like
> that..for a street boy.)

THE MAN IN THE CAR SPEEDS OFF.

> GARY
> Alright then, asshole!

VIEW of Mike's sleeping face.

INSIDE OF MIKE's thoughts. He is flying over the city
streets, *above the Mercedes Benz, effortlessly hovering
and gliding above it, between the buildings.   Like a
bird.*

Mike wakes and looks at Scottie, who is talking to
Gary.

MIKE'S THOUGHTS

The first time I met Scott, I had a feeling he was a sort of comic book hero. He was always saying the right thing at the right moment, and standing up for me when there was no reason to. Look at his face now, when the sunlight shines off his lower lip, like it is the face of some sort of statue. Strong and soft at the same time. I never could figure out what Scott was doing here with us on the street in the first place, like he was on some sort of crusade, to help the poor. Because he really did come from a rich Portland family. I know because he brought me to his house one day and showed me around. I mean, wow, they were rich! They even had a swimming pool. Scott's the only kid that I had ever met that had a swimming pool. I'd make a bet with anybody right now, that Scott is a saint or a hero, or some such higher placed person.

*M*eanwhile...

Gary and Ray are talking. Ray, who is a Chicano street kid, is looking poetically off into the distance.

RAY

My father was a gaucho. But nobody gonna find him. He killed a guy and split. Nobody gonna find that fuck. I never gonna find him.

Ray spits into the gutter and the spit drifts in a small stream made by the shop-owner who was washing his windows, down the street and into a drainage grating.

View of MIKE as he closes his eyes, oblivious to what is going on around him.

*T*he music in a DISCO blares, at night, and all we can see is Mike's face, sleeping. The disco MUSIC STOPS, and the lights go up.

A broom passes by Mike's head.

Finally, THE MANAGER'S SHOES appear at his head.

> MANAGER (o.s.)
> What's wrong with him?   Passed out?

The shoes prod Mike.

> MANAGER (o.s.)
> Hey, wake up.

Mike wakes up in a WARD ROOM BED in the daytime.
He looks around him. The room has a lot of light,
windows practically on all sides of the room.   There are
other DETOX men and women in other beds.   Mike gets
up and starts to walk out, but he is wearing a gown.

A nurse stops him.

> NURSE
> Excuse me.   Are you all right?

> MIKE
> Yeah.   I'm fine. (Mike looks around the room.)

> NURSE
> If you're going to leave us, it's okay, but we
> need you to sign out, and you'll need to get
> your clothes from downstairs.

> MIKE
> Oh.   Yeah. (he pauses and looks around the
>   place.)
> Do you live here?

> NURSE
> Why...no.   But sometimes I feel like I do.

The nurse walks him over to a clipboard on a desk.
Mike signs the board, and she gives him a receipt.

MIKE
What's this?

NURSE
That's just a receipt.   You can throw it away
if you don't want it.   That's what most people
do with it.

Then we cut to Mike's face at night. As his eyes open
he takes a look around him, a little dazed, trying to
figure where he is. We see he is under a store awning.
A lot of fog is rolling across the street.

A twenty-eight-year-old woman stops in a Mercedes
Benz sedan, similar to the one that the German man
was driving. She motions Mike to get inside the car.

Dazed, Mike looks at the car, then responds.

MIKE
This chick is living in a new car ad.

Inside a hallway entrance to the woman's home, Mike
and the woman take off their jackets.

MIKE
This is like a dream.   A pretty woman never
picks me up.

Mike begins to caress her arm.

LADY
They Don't?   Well.   I Don't see why not...

MIKE
Is this your house?

LADY (caressing his head)
Yes...

Mike follows the woman into her...

L iving room where sit Scottie and Gary on a plush sofa. Mike sees them.

                    MIKE
          Oh...

Mike sits down in an easy chair next to the sofa.

                    MIKE
          What's up, Gary? Scottie?

                    GARY
          HEY, DUDE.

                    LADY
          You men make yourselves comfortable, and I'll
          be right back. There're cokes in the
          refrigerator — help yourself.

They watch her go.

                    SCOTTIE
          She's cool. She just likes to have three guys,
          'cause — it takes her a little while to get
          warmed up. It's normal. Nothing kinky.

                    MIKE
          Oh.

Mike looks around the room. Gary leans closer to
Mike.

                    GARY
          Hey, did you get into that Van Halen concert
          last night?

                    MIKE
          I've never been to a concert, dude.

Interior of the Woman's bedroom. Mike undresses. He waits by the side of the bed and takes a last drag on a cigarette and puts it out. Then the woman arrives, lets down her negligé and approaches Mike like an EARTH MOTHER, slowly, big breasted, warm, comforting.

As she approaches, Mike begins to see a familiar face. He is upset when he looks into her eyes. And he begins to spasmodically shake then he grows sleepy, and finally, as she is upon him, he passes out.

Outside, Gary and Scottie struggle with Mike's body.

They plop Mike down on the corner, under a streetlight, fold his arms under his stomach and bend him over so he is sitting up against the light pole.

> SCOTT
> (putting money into his pocket)
> He always does this! I'm surprised he makes money at all.

> GARY
> How do we tell if he's okay?

> SCOTT
> Well, he's not dead.

Scott listens to his heart.

> SCOTT
> Listen.

Gary listens.

> SCOTT
> He's not dead. He's just passed out. It's a condition. It's called narcolepsy.

> GARY
> Scared the shit out of her. What causes it. Sex?

> SCOTT
Stress. Some hustler, huh?

Silence for a second.

> GARY
Where are we going to take him?

Scott lifts Mike's body up and carries him to a soft
carpet of grass on the edge of a lawn. Scott looks
around to see if it is okay. Then he speaks to Mike
even though he is asleep.

> SCOTT
Hey, little brother. You stay here, and when
you wake up, just come back into town. I'll
be there waiting for you. I figure you're going
to be safer here in this comfy neighborhood
than in the city. I grew up in a neighborhood
like this. It'll be safe here.

Scottie hides a tear. Then he takes his jacket off and
puts it over Mike, then leaves him there.

*M*ike's face is lying down with his nose pressed
against a leafy ground in the daytime.

He wakes up, stands, makes his way up a slope and
out to the street. He brushes himself off as the
Mercedes Benz shows up again. Mike recognizes it, and
walks up to the window of the car. It is the MAN,
though, not the lady. The Man speaks with a German
accent – and he is about 35 years old. HIS NAME IS
HANS.

> MIKE
Hi.

> Hans
Say....

Hans reads Mike's shirt.

                    Hans
        Say, Bill. What's happening?

Mike brushes himself off and walks down the road,
thinking that the guy is weird.

                    MIKE
        Nothing much.

Hans drives alongside Mike in his car.

                    Hans
        Do you want a lift? Bill?

                    MIKE
        Hey, isn't this the lady's car?

                    Hans
        Is Alena a friend of yours?   She's a friend of
        mine. Any friend of Alena's is a friend of
        mine. Do you want to be my friend?

                    MIKE
        Not really.

                    Hans
        Get in and I'll take you someplace. Yes?
        Where do you want to go?

Mike doesn't respond, and walks on.

He pauses a moment, and looks at the houses in the
neighborhood. He looks down the street and can see
Hans stopped in his car. The guy gets out, and leans
against the car.

                    MIKE
        This guy is a pervert. I can tell.

To Hans:

                    MIKE
        Go home!

THE HOUSES LINE THE STREET, EACH WITH A LITTLE
CALIFORNIA STYLE GARDEN. MIKE CAN SEE ALL THE
ROOFS OF THE HOUSES LIFT OFF, AND THE FURNITURE
INSIDE EACH HOUSE FLY OUT AND CIRCLE IN THE AIR.
MIKE GETS THE JITTERS AND PASSES OUT.

THE MERCEDES BENZ PULLS UP NEXT TO HIS HEAD, WHICH
IS NOW ON THE GROUND.

P O R t L A n d

When Mike wakes up he is in Scottie's arms. They sit
under a statue in a park. The statue is of two Indians
pointing out across the horizon, and on the base of the
statue is written: *The Coming of the White Man.*

Mike looks at Scott and then at the new surroundings.

At the Broadway Cafe Mike bites into a hamburger.

> MIKE
> How'd we get home?

> SCOTT
> That German guy. Hans. He brought you
> downtown, you were passed out. He said he
> was heading to Portland, so I asked him for a
> ride.

> MIKE
> I don't remember any German guy.

> SCOTT
> Well. You were sleeping.

> MIKE
> How much do you make off me while I'm
> sleeping?

> SCOTT
> Just a ride, Mike. I don't make anything.
> What, you think that I sell your body while
> you are asleep.

> MIKE
> Yeah.

Scott sips from a coffee cup.

                    SCOTT
          No, Mike. I'm on your side.

He puts down the cup. Mike knows Scottie always tells
the truth. Mike is a little embarrassed, that he has
maybe offended Scott's honor.

                    MIKE
          I was just kidding, dude.

                    SCOTT
          Gary's up here somewhere. He left three days
          ago, he flew up with some John.

                    MIKE
          Exotic. Have you seen your dad?

                    SCOTT
          Are you kidding?

                    MIKE
          I'd visit my dad, if he was here.

                    SCOTT
          I have to take care of you.

                    MIKE
          How about your mom?

                    SCOTT
          No.

                    MIKE
          That lady. She looked like. My mother.

                    SCOTT
          Is that why you passed out?

                    MIKE
          Yeah. I mean. I don't know. She really
          looked like my mother. I must have been
          imagining things.

A pause.

The Broadway Cafe is beginning to pick up in business.
The table where Scott and Mike sit is in front of a large
window, and it is semi-circular in shape. Scottie spies
Gary across the street.

He bounds up out of his chair and Mike watches him as
he goes to the door, kicks it open and yells to Gary.

                              SCOTT
                    HEY! You dick!!

Gary sees Scott and runs across the street.

*L*ater in the BROADWAY CAFE, there are other street
kids hanging around the table.

Scott has his arm around a girl named DENISE, who has
a lot of make up on and long stringy hair and who
carries a teddy bear. Denise is crying and Scott is
consoling her.

                    MIKE'S THOUGHTS:
          It was almost as if Scott was on some sort of
          crusade or mission, when you checked him
          out.   He could make you feel good right at the
          very time that you felt so bad. I remember
          there were many times that I had been
          sobbing in Scott's arms and he was helping me
          out too. He was the great protector of us all,
          and the great planner. He gave us hope in the
          future. Even though there was no future.
          There must have been real trouble at home,
          though, for Scott not to want to visit his
          father.

Scott strokes Denise's hair adoringly and gives her a kiss
every now and then.

Mike looks across the table at CARL, a skinny kid with
black hair and a large floppy sports cap, and GARY,
who is talking with him.

> MIKE'S THOUGHTS
> That's Carl. He's always around the
> Broadway, he didn't run away from home like
> a lot of these kids did. He had a mom, and no
> dad, at least they didn't know where he was.
> And one day, he came home to the apartment
> where they lived, and there was no mom
> anymore either. He didn't know where she
> went. That was six months ago.

MARY, an older, wiser street prostitute who is chain
smoking Kool cigarettes.

> MIKE'S THOUGHTS
> That's Mary over there. She was a mean old
> chick. She was maybe thirty now. Old, old.
> Somebody once told me that in the past, Mary
> had this enemy, a chick that had turned her
> in. And Mary had gone off and kicked this
> chick to death right in the street in front of
> everybody. I don't know if it's true, but I
> watched out, just in case. I was afraid of
> Mary. And everyone else was too.

Mary takes a drag from her cigarette and blows smoke
in Mike's face.

Scott notices this. But he attends to Denise's problems.

> MIKE's THOUGHTS
> (as he coughs)
> This was our little round table, a point around
> which everything else revolved. It was our
> "center." It was like our home. Our living
> room. Not everyone was the best of friends,
> but everyone knew everyone else, and we kind
> of stuck together.

*M*ike on the street. He watches as a man carrying a
large bag of tin cans, crosses at a crosswalk. Mike steps
up to him and begins walking. His name is MARTY.

MIKE
Hey Marty. What's goin' on?

MARTY
Is that you Mike? Hey, what's new with you?
You look pretty good.

MIKE
How many you got so far today?

MARTY
I reckon that I picked up about twenty-three
bucks so far with these cans, and some I got
stashed back in the bushes. You know the old
hiding place?

MIKE
Wow!

MARTY
Don't tell anybody, though. Just between you
and me. You need a place to stay?

MIKE
I always need a place to stay, dude.

MARTY
Yeah, well, I'm under the bridge. You can
join me if you like.

MIKE
Yeah, I think I'll rooftop it tonight. I'm
hanging with a friend.

MARTY
Am I walking too fast for you?

MIKE
No, but I'll see you around. See you under the
bridge.

MARTY
Okay, Mike.

Mike stops walking with the guy and he splits down the street at a fast clip.

*I*nside the BROADWAY CAFE, Mike smokes a cigarette at the round table and watches Gary and Carl playing keep-away with Denise's teddy bear. Denise is swearing, using profanities that are unusual for a girl.

*N*ight. Mike walks through a dark wet troubled inner-city alley and on the other side, there is a parked car. In the car sits a man in his 40's, bestial, good looking but overweight. He beeps his car horn at Mike.

Mike pauses, lights a cigarette coolly and walks to the car and leans in the window.

                    MIKE
          Hey - what's up?

*I*nt. MOTEL, nightime.

The man is naked in the background standing in front of a mirror in a motel bathroom, as Mike sits naked on a bed in front of a t.v. set laughing at the show that is on.

We see various *still compositions* of the two making love.

A field. Day. Two figures cross the field. One is Bob Pigeon, a man in his fifties, and the other, his manservant, Budd. Because of his girth, Bob has problems crossing the field.

                    BUDD
          Jesus...the things we've seen...do you
          remember a thing since we moved from
          graffitti bridge?

                    BOB
          No more of that, Budd.

                    BUDD
          Ha-ha, what a crazy night.

*W*ay above the two walking figures, Gary wakes near
a heating duct atop a ten story building. He yawns,
looks down at the street and spies Bob and Budd.

GARY'S VIEW: a tiny Bob and Budd are making their
way across a field.

                    GARY
          Hey, Scottie, here comes that fat pig himself!!!
          He owes me money!

Scottie, atop an adjacent building peeks his head over
the edge. The two guys are relatively close to one
another but far from the street.

                    SCOTT
          Who?

                    GARY
          You know, the fat one...Pigeon!

                    SCOTT
          He stole my shoes, the dick!

                    GARY
          Hey, everybody, here comes Bob the chisler!

He yells to the other buildings and other street kids to
wake up. Scottie pours an old paper cup of Coca-Cola
over Bob and Budd below.

                    GARY
          Look out, it's raining Coke!

Bob hears the show atop the buildings.

> BOB
> Ah, I think my friends can see I am back from
> Boise.

Bob looks worried and happy at the same time, not
knowing if they are friend or foe. He shields himself
from the Coke sprinkles.

> BOB
> Do you see any clouds in the sky, Budd?

> BUDD
> No, Bob.

The Derelict Hotel.

Budd and Bob enter the threshold of a busted up but
operating hotel. There is a fire in a trashcan turned
upside down, with holes poked in it.

Budd looks around the hotel.

> BUDD
> Is Jane Lightwork alive, Bob?

> BOB
> She's alive, Budd.

> BUDD
> Is she holding on?

> BOB
> Old...old, Budd.

> BUDD
> She must be old, she has no choice...

THE TWO sit at a larger fire deeper into the derelict
hotel.

                    BUDD
I remember her daughter, she died years
ago...of old age. She must be old, all right.
That was before I came to Clements Inn.

                    BOB
(warming by the fire)
Ahh...

                    BUDD
Jesus...the things that we've seen. Aren't I
right, Bob? Aren't I right?

                    BOB
We have seen the light at the end of the
tunnel...

                    BUDD
That we have, that we have...in fact Bob, we
have. Jesus...the things that we've seen.

$\mathcal{S}$cott drinks from a beer can inside the derelict hotel,
tosses it to a young boy, laughs, wipes his mouth and
puts his lit cigarette into the mouth of Gary, making
his way to some steps, through a circle of girls, kisses
Denise, who we remember from the Broadway Cafe, and
charges up the steps.

Inside the hotel on a staircase landing, Scottie passes a
couple of figures, one is asleep and one is awake.

                    SCOTTIE
Where's Bob?

                    A BOY
Fast asleep.

                    BUDD
And he's snoring like a horse.

SCOTTIE OPENS A DOOR AT THE TOP OF THE STEPS AND WALKS INTO A ROOM, INTERRUPTING MIKE, WHO STANDS OVER BOB'S SNORING BODY.

Mike coolly holds up a wad of bills and a folded envelope of cocaine.

>   MIKE
>   I picked his pocket.

>   SCOTTIE (whispering)
>   What did you get, dude?

>   MIKE
>   Just this.

Scottie takes the cocaine from him, sits down at the foot of the bed and begins to undfold the packet. Bob turns in the bed and the rush of air from the sheets blows the white powder out of the packet.

>   BOB
>   What the hell?

Mike laughs.

>   BOB
>   What time is it, son?

>   SCOTTIE (climbing in bed with
>   Bob)
>   What do you care?

Bob, dazed, is looking around himself, like he is being had.

>   SCOTTIE (amusing Mike)
>   Why, you wouldn't even look at a clock,
>   unless hours were lines of coke, dials looked
>   like the signs of gay bars, or time itself was a
>   fair hustler in black leather... isn't that right,
>   dude?

Bob staggers out of bed wretching and spitting. Then back into his waking stupor, feeling something is being put over on him.

SCOTT
There's no reason to know the time. We are timeless.

Bob checks his wallet.

BOB
Aren't you forgetting, Scottie my boy, [A GOVERNOR'S SON], that we who steal, do so at midnight?

Bob' s money and cocaine are gone. Bob turns angry and bellows.

BOB
What the...who ripped me off? Budd!!! Budd!!!!

Stairs again.

BUDD
Yes, Bob!!!

Budd stands at the stoop and comes through the door, just as Bob is running out.

BOB
I fell asleep and have been robbed!

BUDD
Jane!!!

The room below.

Jane Lightwork, the owner of the established hotel,
comes to arms. She is very old.

>   JANE
>   You'd think that I could keep the peace in my
>   house...

B_{edroom.}

Scottie and Mike laugh. Mike gets down on his hands
and knees and tries to scoop up a little cocaine from
the floor.

H_{all.}

>   JANE
>   Bob, Bob we'll find your drugs. We'll find
>   them.

A_{nother hall.}

Bob is storming down it in a rage, people opening doors
of the rooms.

>   BOB
>   Jane, I know you well enough...

Y_{et another hall.}

Hotel dwellers are watching Jane move down the hall
answering Bob.

>   JANE
>   I know you, Bob... you owe me money, Bob,
>   and now you pick a fight with me, and are
>   disturbing the peace of my hotel.

MAIN derelict hall of the hotel.

Bob parades, in his night clothes, in front of a
gathering of outcasts in the hotel.

> BOB
> This hotel is full of thieves...junkies!

> JANE
> You are the thief!

> BOB
> They picked my pocket!

LAUGHTER from the throngs of outcasts. Jane enters a
balcony overlook of the main hall. Mike and Scott
enter, arms around each other, laughing.

> JANE
> It's impossible to board a dozen or so men and
> women who live honestly and have the others
> live like junkies.

One of the dwellers listening to the argument is shooting
up as they speak. We see a close view of the needle
and Bob running around in the background.

Bob makes his way next to Scott.

> BOB
> You have corrupted me, Scottie, I was an
> innocent before I met you...and now look at
> me...just a little better than wicked. I used
> to be a virtuous man...

Scottie is laughing at him.

> BOB
> ...well, virtuous enough. I swore a little. I
> never gambled more than seven times a week.
> Poker. I never picked up a street boy more
> than once a quarter...

Scottie laughs.

> BOB
> ...of an hour. Bad company has corrupted
> me. I'll be darned if I haven't forgotten what
> the inside of a church looks like.

> MIKE
> Where do you find your strike tonight, Bob?

> SCOTTIE
> I see a good change for Bob to make. From
> Stealing to Preaching.

> BOB
> Stealing is my vocation, Scott. It's not a sin
> for a man to labor at his vocation.

> GARY
> Hey...psst...

The three gather around Gary.

> GARY
> Very early tomorrow morning, there will be
> small time rock and roll promoters coming
> back from their show. Every night, they walk
> home with the loot and they stop by the Grotto
> Bar, one mile away from here, and more often
> than not they've been drinking already. If we
> can't steal from them on their way to the bar,
> we can get them when they come out. See,
> dude?

> MIKE
> I'm not gonna rob anybody.   I'd rather sell
> my ass. Straight and simple. It's less risky.

> BOB
> So long as I don't know these guys
> personally...it's okay with me.

> GARY
> They're from Beaverton. New to the
> business...

> **MIKE**
> Not me. I'm not going along on this crackpot
> scheme. Especially since Gary thought it up.

> **BOB**
> Come off it, Mikey. Find a better way to
> make a buck. Something to fall back on,
> other than your ass.

> **MIKE**
> Scott's inheritance.

Bob walks away from the two others.

> **SCOTT**
> (whispering)
> Come along, Mikey. I have a joke I wanna
> play...a joke I can't pull off alone...

Mike laughs and joins Bob, hugging him around his fat
belly.

> **BOB**
> Oh, my sweetheart, come and rob with us
> tomorrow.

> **MIKE**
> I was going to come anyway.

SCOTT hugs the others too.

> **MIKE**
> We'll be rich!!!

Scottie dances away.

> **SCOTT**
> Provide for us, oh great psychedelic Papa!

Scottie grabs Denise and kisses her then begins to leave
through the door. He throws her to Mike who catches
her and runs off with her.

> **Scottie**
> Good catch dude...and meet me on three
> street!

Scott leaves, Bob follows him:

Outside the derelict hotel.

> BOB
> Scott. When you inherit your fortune, on
> your twenty-first birthday, let's see...how far
> away is this?

> SCOTT
> One week away, Bob, just one more week.

> BOB
> Let's not call ourselves robbers, but Diannah's
> foresters. Gentlemen of the shade. Minions of
> the Moon. Men of good government.

> SCOTT
> (under his breath)
> When I turn twenty-one, I don't want any
> more of this life. My mother and father will
> be surprised at the incredible change. It will
> impress them more when such a fuck up like
> me turns good than if I had been a good son
> all along. All the past years I will think of as
> one big vacation. At least it wasn't as boring
> as schoolwork. All my bad behavior I'm going
> to throw away to pay my debt. I will change
> when everybody expects it the least.

Scott turns and leaves.

> BOB
> And you will become a hard roller, a hatchet
> man for your old man.

Scott laughs to himself, because he knows Bob is
misunderstanding him. Bob is part of the past life that
he says he is going to throw away.

> SCOTT
> No! You will be the hatchet man, Bob, that
> will be your job, and so there will rarely be a
> job hatcheted. It will be one big endless party,
> won't it?

Bob laughs. Scott walks across a field.

> BOB
> Well, at least my little friend has offered me a
> job. They are so good to me.

*I*nside the Broadway Cafe. Day.

Denise and Mike hang out together. Both are smoking
cigarettes which have made a billow of smoke that
hangs over the table that is in the front window.

> DENISE
> Moms are great, because, you know, I could
> always go to my mom and say, hey I need a
> new lipstick, and she would always give me
> money for that. That was great.

> MIKE
> I only saw my mom once, but I remember
> what she looked like. She was very beautiful.

> DENISE
> What do you mean, once?

> MIKE
> When I was born.

> DENISE
> How could you remember when that god-awful
> thing happened?

> MIKE
> Dunno. But I remember it. Yeah, I remember
> how beautiful and kind she was. She was
> good.

> DENISE
> And she split from you, huh?

> MIKE
> Maybe she didn't mean to.

>   DENISE
> Did you see what was going on, Mike? Between
> Pinky and Dale? Did you see that? That's the
> third fight I've seen today. Things always
> happen in threes.

>   MIKE
> I don't know. They have a sort of, ah,
> relationship. Between them.

Across the street there are three people, a TALL MAN,
who has his hat stuck on his boot and a lady and
another man with a dog on a leash.

>   MIKE
> I don't know about that, but, ah, listen, what
> you and me talk about, it's just between us,
> you understand? Hey, what's over there, see
> those assholes? Who are they, you know any
> of them?

>   DENISE
> I can't see that far.

DENISE STANDS AND OPENS THE FRONT DOOR AND YELLS
ACROSS THE STREET.

>   DENISE
> HEY!

The group across the street look up and begin yelling
back, but we cannot hear them.

*U*nder the Burnside Bridge, day.

Mike and Denise kiss, and their arms are entagled in a
loving, but awkward embrace. Twigs and leaves are
caught in Denise's hair as they are lying on the ground.

Different STILL COMPOSITIONS OF SEX while they are
lying in the wilds under the bridge.

Then...

Denise lights a cigarette.

                    DENISE
          That reminds me, I gotta send my Ma a
          Christmas card, I still haven't done it yet.

                    MIKE
          Yeah, I haven't done it either.

                    DENISE
          Your mom lives in Idaho right now?

                    MIKE
          Yeah.

                    DENISE
          I used to live in Montana.

                    MIKE
          My own cousin. He's dead. And my grandma,
          that's one...two...it usually comes in threes.

                    DENISE
          Does come in threes.

                    MIKE
          My cousin died, my grandmother died, and
          right after she died, her daughter died. My
          aunt. Within a year. And they wuz all
          women, not even a year, six...well....six
          months-eight months, three women in the
          family died.

A pause.

                    MIKE
          That's funny, huh? I WONDER WHY YOU
          THOUGHT THAT, cuz, my FATHER says stuff like
          that.

                    DENISE
          Well, my grandma was superstitious.

 MIKE
My father told me that, said things usually
come in threes...and I said, aw....you're
crazy.

A Long pause. A motorcycle passes, someone yells, and
a horn honks.

 MIKE
It sounds crazy. That's my lucky number too.

 DENISE
Huh?

 MIKE
Three.

 DENISE
Mine's eight.

 MIKE
I like three.

 DENISE
You know why I like eight?

 MIKE
Why?

 DENISE
Cause of the eight ball. You know. When
you're stuck behind the eight ball? I fuckin'
feel stuck behind the eight ball today, I'll tell
you. The business is so slow in the middle of
the week, you know that Mike?

*P*ublic bathroom. Night.

Mike empties the contents of his pockets at a bathroom
sink. He has in his possession: One condom. One comb
with blond hair stuck in it. One nickel. Half a stick of
gum. One knife with the letter W stamped on it.

He arranges these things in a neat order on the surface
of the sink while a man flushes a toilet in the
background and uses another sink. Mike is quite at
home here. He takes his time arranging the articles,
and washing his hands. He looks over at the man
washing his hands and gives him a friendly smile.

The man leaves. Mike puts all the things on the sink
into his pockets. Then he walks over to a urinal,
unzips his fly and starts to take a leak. A shadow
opens the door in back of him, and without turning
around, Mike senses the presence of a man.

*A*lleyway. Night.

Scottie is helping Bob with a disguise, putting on pants
over a large belly, with medallions around the neck.

> SCOTT
> How long has it been, Bob, since you could see
> your own feet?

> BOB
> About four years, Scottie. Four years of
> grief. It blows a man up like a balloon.

Mike and Budd appear, running, with costumes on.
There are two others behind them.

> MIKE
> There's rock and roll money walking this way!

> BUDD
> And they're drunk as skunks.

> MIKE
> This is going to be easy. We can do it lying
> down.

> SCOTT
> But don't fall asleep, now, Mike.

                    BUDD
Shh!! Here they come!

                    SCOTT
You four should head them off there!

                    BOB
We four? How many are walking with them?

                    MIKE
About six.

                    BOB
Huh, shouldn't they be robbing us?

Scottie laughs. Bob waddles along the side of the
alleyway, stepping on a curb, then in a pothole losing
his balance. Another accomplice whistles from atop a
building. We SEE the group of ROCK AND ROLL
promoters.

Bob walks further from Mike and Scottie.

                    SCOTTIE
If they escape from you, we'll get them here.

Bob struggles as he walks.

                    BOB
Eight feet of cobblestones is like 30 yards of flat
road with me.

Mike and Scott run off, laughing at him.

                    BOB
I can't see a damned thing in here.

                    BUDD
Jesus, will you shut up! And keep on your
toes!

Budd sees the promoters coming and waves to Bob as he
lies down on the ground.

                    BUDD
Lie down!!

                        BOB
        Lie down!?

                        BUDD
        Lie down and stay quiet, until they round the
        corner and we'll ambush them.

                        BOB
        Have you got a crane to lift me up again?

Budd laughs.

                        MIKE
        They're coming!!

*D*own the way, the rock and roll promoters are
approaching, having no knowledge of the buffoonery at
the other end of the tunneling alleyway. They are
drunk.

                        VICTIM 1
        Come along neighbor, Tommy will lead the
        way. I've lost track of time...(burp)

*A*t the other end of the alley:

Bob and three others are marching in procession,
chanting, a facsimile of Rashneesh, but a bad act.

The rock promoters approach, smashing a bottle.

                        VICTIM 1
        Who are these jokers?

                        VICTIM 2
        Rashneesh, listen!

          VICTIM 1
   They're chanting....

Scottie and Mike hide behind garbage cans, laughing.

The rock promoters circle the group of chanting
Rashneesh.

          VICTIM 3
   I thought that all you Rashneesh had up and
   left...

Victim 1 pours a beer on one of their heads. Just as he
does this Bob pulls out two long pistols, almost heavy
enough that he cannot hold them straight, barrels
parallel.

          BOB
   Aha! One move and I'll blow you away, you
   sully scumbags, up against that wall!

One of the victims falls down and begins to run away.
One of Bob's men starts after him. A lockbox that he
was carrying falls to the ground. Bob spies it.

          BOB
   No! Let him go!

Bob aims one pistol at the running figure as he keeps
the others against the wall with the other pistol. He
fires three times. One of Bob's boys grabs the lockbox.

A VIEW of the running figure, bullets cutting around
him.

          BOB
   Look at him go!

          VICTIM 2
   Don't shoot us!

Bob winks at the lockbox and shoots the gun in the air.

All the rock promoters go running. Bob charges after
them, firing the gun twice more in the air, then once
at the lockbox, breaking it open.

                    BOB
        The valise is open. Let's see what we got.

Mike and Scottie hiding behind trashcans.

                    SCOTTIE
        Where are our disguises?

Mike runs to his stash and finds two large capes and
large hats. They put these on.

Bob finds wads of money and receipts.

                    BOB
        Ticket anyone? To next week's show?

He throws these on the ground and the boys fall over
themselves for the tickets. Bob wads the money and
puts it back in the box, laughing to himself.

Mike and Scottie sneak closer to the group still hiding,
long flowing capes concealing their identity.

                    BOB
        Scott and Mike have disappeared, did the shots
        scare them away?

They sneak closer. Mike lights a big firecracker and
waits.

                    BOB
        ...maybe we should get the hell out of here.
        But, are they such chickens?

A LOUD EXPLOSION!

Mike and Scottie, disguised, jump out with large silver
baseball bats, swinging them and making as much noise
as they can, knocking over a set of garbage cans,
flashing flashlights into Bob and the others' eyes.

Frightened, Bob drops the lockbox and runs, the others
follow, Mike and Scottie hitting them with the bats as
they go.

                    BOB
        Get the box! Oh, fuck!

Mike swings the bat at Bob, it grazes the side of a
building and sparks fly from it. Bob wheezes from the
run.

Scottie chases the others in the same direction.

They stand, kicking garbage cans and watching them
run, convulsing with laughter.

                  SCOTTIE
        The thieves scatter!

                   MIKE
        Bob Pigeon will sweat to death!

*J*ack Favor enters the Governor's CHAMBERS day.

                   JACK
        Can anyone tell me about my son?

He walks across the room.

                   JACK
        It's been a full three months since I last saw
        him. Where is my son Scott?

                   AID
        We don't know, sir.

                   JACK
        Ask around in Old Town, in some of the
        taverns there. Some say he frequently is seen
        down there drinking with street denizens.
        Some who they say even rob our citizens and
        store owners. I can't believe that such an
        effeminate boy supports such "friends."

A high overhead (helicopter?) view of the country landscape in the early morning. Far below us on a lonely road is a small dot, a motorcycle, traveling east.

*F*urther along on its travels, the motorcycle crosses a steel BRIDGE.

*O*ld Town day.

Scottie and Mike, riding on a stolen motorcycle, sweep through the early morning streets without being noticed.

*S*topping at a stop light in the city.

Scott pauses to think.

> SCOTT
> Mikey, do you realize how long I have been here out on the streets, on this crusade?

> MIKE
> About as long as the rest of us. I mean. I can't even remember that far back, Scott, I mean......

> SCOTT
> It's been three years, Mike.

> MIKE
> Wow...that's a really long time, Scott. Have I been here three years, too?

> SCOTT
> What I'm getting at, Mike, is that we are survivors.

                    MIKE
Yeah, well, so, isn't that obvious?

                    SCOTT
Yes. It is incredibly obvious. They could drop
a bomb on this city and you know what we
would do?

                    MIKE
      (thinking)
DIE?

                    SCOTT
No. We would survive. Because we are _____.

                    MIKE
Survivors!

                    SCOTT
Right, Mike.

                    MIKE
Say, Scott. Whaddya say we go survive over
at the Broadway Cafe a little bit, at least it's
warm over there.

*I*nt. Broadway Cafe. Day.

Mike and Scott sit around the table with Carl and Mary.
Mike blows a smoke ring.

Denise runs in the door of the cafe, excited about
something.

                    DENISE
MIKE! Scottie! There's a man from City Hall
down the street. He wants to speak with you,
Scottie.

                    SCOTT
What's that?

                    DENISE
He says that he's sent by your father.

> SCOTT
> Say hello and send him to my mother.

> MIKE
> What kind of a man is it?

> DENISE
> A young man. And he's got cops with him.

> SCOTT
> Cops....

*S*treet exterior day.

Two POLICEMEN and one OFFICIAL are walking down the street toward the Broadway cafe.

*B*roadway Cafe interior day.

The cops enter, passing The PROPRIETOR of the cafe, an aging heavyset woman named NANCY.

> NANCY
> Good morning, officers...

> COP 2
> How are you this morning, NANCY? Don't mind if we take a look around your place, do you?

One officer is already inspecting the stolen motorcycle outside.

Mike sees this, and looks the other way from the cop who is peering in the Broadway cafe window.

> COP 1
> Have you seen the young Scott Favor?

> NANCY
> I do believe he was here just a second ago.

Nancy looks in the front window.

> NANCY
> Oh, yeah, there he is.

Nancy points Scott out.

Scott is giving Denise a long kiss, hiding from the cops.

The OFFICIAL walks to the front window of the Cafe.

Scott pretends he is being rudely interrupted.

> SCOTT
> Ah-ha...what have we here?

> OFFICIAL
> Excuse me...Mr. Favor...we have been sent in
> search of a fat man...a large bearded....

> COP 3
> ...FAT MAN...

> COP 2
> Goes by Bob Pigeon.

> SCOTT
> Bob Pigeon?

> COP 1
> That's right.

> SCOTT
> What do you want with him?

> COP 2
> Ahem. There's been a report, sir, he has been
> involved in a holdup...

> COP 1
> Last night. Have you seen him?

                    SCOTT
I saw him around last night, when was the
 holdup?

                    COP 1
Late. Two in the morning.

                    SCOTT
I saw him about four, but he wasn't very loose
with his wallet. Did he get away with any of
the money?

                    COP 2
Yes, indeed, sir...two thousand dollars of a
rock promoter's money.

                    SCOTT
Well, anyway, I haven't seen him <u>recently</u>.
Why do you look here?

                    COP 1
They say he has friends here.

                    SCOTTIE
I beg your pardon.

                    COP 2
Sorry...

                    OFFICIAL
Sorry for the interruption. We have a
message for you from your father. He says
that he would like to see you as soon as
possible.

THE OFFICIAL HANDS SCOTT AN ENVELOPE.

                    SCOTT
Thank you for your message.

Scott takes the envelope and puts it on the table.

$\mathcal{S}$treet, day.

The police close the door.

> COP 1
> Hmmm.

> COP 2
> What about the dead body.

> COP 1
> Let's not get Favor's kid involved in this report
> if we can help it. But if he were my son,
> I'd....

Cop 1 makes a fist and slams it in the palm of his other
hand.

INT. Broadway Cafe.

> MIKE
> Bob is a wanted man now.

> SCOTTIE
> And as dangerous to be around as cops
> themselves.

> MIKE
> We need a hiding place.

> SCOTTIE
> Where should we go?

> MIKE
> To visit my brother.

> SCOTT
> You have a brother?

> MIKE
> Yes, I have one.

SCOTT
Where is he?

MIKE
He's in........he's in.......

Mike suddenly begins to shake, and, falls asleep.

Scottie picks up the envelope from his father and puts
it in his pocket.

I d A h o

Mike and Scott are stuck on a long straight road in the desert. Mike is angry at Scott because he doesn't think he knows how the motorcycle works.

Scott is trying again and again to start the engine.

> MIKE
> Come on...

> SCOTT
> Shut up, Mike.

He tries to turn it over again.

> SCOTT
> If I had known that it was going to be this hard to start, then I wouldn't have stopped it at all.

Mike looks at the road and the surrounding area. It is the same road that he was stuck on in the beginning.

> MIKE
> Scott? I just know that I have been on this road before.

Mike stares at the face in the road. Two cactus for eyes, mountains for hair, a cloud shadow forms the mouth over a red nose road with a dotted line running down it.

At night, Scott and Mike sit next to a fire they have made on the side of the road. We can hear Indians in the distance dancing and chanting a song.

> MIKE
> It sure is lonely out in the desert.

> SCOTT
> Yeah, I guess.

> MIKE
> If I had had a normal family, and a good upbringing, then I would have been a well adjusted person. But somehow that just didn't work out.

> SCOTT
> Depends on what you'd call "normal."

> MIKE
> Well, normal, you know, with a mom and a dad and a dog and shit like that...normal.

> SCOTT
> So you didn't have a dog?   Or you didn't have a dad...

> MIKE
> I didn't have a dog and I didn't have a dad. Well, not a normal dad...

The music is getting louder. It sounds like a war chant.

> MIKE
> Hey Scott?

> SCOTT
> What?

Mike is hesitating. He is about to say something personal. He looks at Scott and back to the fire, a few times too many.

                    SCOTT
What, Mike?

                     MIKE
Oh. Have you ever.   Uh...

Scott is getting Mike's drift.

Mike rubs his crotch.

                     MIKE
I mean, don't you ever get horny?

                    SCOTT
Yeah.   But...

                     MIKE
Oh, yeah...not for a guy.

                    SCOTT
Mike. Two guys can't love each other. They
can only be friends.

An awkward moment passes where Mike is looking away
from Scott and Scott can't help but look at Mike. Then
Scott catches Mike's eye and motions for him to come
closer to him.

Mike walks over to Scott and Scott holds him in his
arms.

Overhead VIEW of the two in front of the campfire.

                    SCOTT
I only have sex for money...

Mike starts to get out some money.

                    SCOTT
I can't take your money.

A pause.

                    SCOTT
But we can be close friends.

The next morning. Mike is sleeping. As he opens his eyes, he can see Scott still trying to start the motorcycle.

Mike stands and looks down the road at an approaching State Police Car. Mike, afraid of the police, starts to move into the bushes.

Scott is out of breath trying to start the bike.

> MIKE
>
> Scott, look...

Scott looks in the direction of the police car.

> SCOTT
>
> Looks like this is it.

> MIKE
>
> Yeah.

Scott hits the side of the gas tank of the bike with the palm of his hand.

> SCOTT
>
> Can't get the bike started. Cops are coming.
> Stuck in the middle of nowhere with a stolen
> bike. Yeah, Mike. Looks like this is the end.

The policeman pulls up to them and parks.

The policeman sits in his car for a second and reports into the radio, then he gets out and walks over to the boys.

Mike gets scared and runs into the desert.

The cop stands and watches. Mike has nowhere to go, he is running into an open desert.

The policeman, a full blooded American Indian, seems amused at his power. He looks at Scott then back at Mike, who trips in the desert and falls in a cloud of dust.

                    COP
    What's the matter with him?

                    SCOTT
    I don't know. I guess he doesn't like cops.

                    COP
    Yeah.

                    SCOTT
    That's how it looks.

                    COP
    What are you kids doing out here?

                    SCOTT
    This cycle is one bitch to turn over. But you probably don't know about motorcycles. You aren't a motorcycle cop.

                    COP
    I turned a few.

Scott walks through the desert looking for Mike where he dropped. He picks him up out of the dirt, spit dripping from his sleeping lips, and smacks him in the face.

                    SCOTT
    Wake up, Mikey, the heat's off.

Mike will not wake up.

*W*hen Mike wakes up. He is inside a TRAILER at
night.

Scott is eating sandwiches to his right that are on a
little T.V. tray.

There is MIKE's BROTHER leaning into him on his left.
He looks at Mike offensively. His brother is very good
looking, but looks like he has lost his mind somewhere
down the line. Which is why he lives in the desert in a
trailer, away from people.

                    SCOTT
          Look, Mike. Sandwiches.

                    BROTHER
          Your mother...now she was a right woman.
          She used to be so proud of you...you
          know...she would just beam. And not Jim
          Beam either. If you know what I mean. We
          used to drive for hours to get a look at you. I
          remember, what was it...eighteen years ago?

                    MIKE
          Twenty-one.

                    BROTHER
          Is that how old you are now? I thought you
          wuz younger than that...what? Well anyway,
          we would start off in the morning to see you,
          and it would take an hour to get to the
          institution. You were maybe one year old.
          What? I wasn't proud that you had to live in
          an institution, mind you...but all the same,
          when I would look at you, all the institutional
          walls would come down and we were a family.
          Your mom, me, and you. God knows where
          dad was.

Mike is getting visibly upset. Scott gets up to go to the
bathroom.

Inside the bathroom night.

Scott enters and notices a velvet portrait of a woman
hanging on the wall. Off screen Scott can hear Mike
and his Brother.

> MIKE (o.s.)
> I don't belong to you, DUDE...I'm not yours...

> BROTHER (o.s.)
> (his voice booms out so unexpectedly deep
> and loud that Scott is startled)
> Shut your mouth! Don't you talk back...

His brother hits the table with a crash.

Living room night.

> BROTHER
> Well...(takes a breath)
> Anyway. You were maybe not in the
> biological sense, my brother, but in our
> business, bro... (holds his hands up in the air)
> And if I'm not your brother, how's come you
> turned out exactly like me then?

Mike has gotten the jitters and fallen asleep in front of
him.

Scott enters from the bathroom.

> BROTHER
> Oh, he'll come out of it. It's like this
> whenever we get together. It's always like
> this when we get together. It's the way that
> we say hello to each other.

He holds his head down.

                    BROTHER
          I'm all that he's got. But he doesn't want me.
          He doesn't care. He'd rather live out on the
          streets. I love him, though.

Scott looks around the trailer at all the velvet portraits
hanging on the walls.

                    BROTHER
          Oh. I paint these for a living. But sometimes
          the people don't send the check when they get
          finished. So I keep them. I like them.

Ext. Trailer. Night.

Mike and his brother sip iced tea. Colored lights
decorate the trailer.

                    BROTHER
          Want me to tell you what happened to your
          Mom? Have you ever heard it? Did you ever
          hear what the hell happened to her?

                    MIKE
          No. But I don't care.

                    BROTHER
          You loved her, and don't tell me you didn't. I
          know you did.

                    MIKE
          I didn't even know her.

                    BROTHER
          Yeah, you loved her, though.

                    MIKE
          I already heard what happened to her.

                    BROTHER
          But you don't know the whole story. One
          thing about the truth. It's interesting.

                    MIKE
          I don't care.

BROTHER
If you had known her, you would care. She
would see guys on the side. At night. When I
wouldn't be around...maybe I'd be in San
Francisco or some darned place, doing my own
business. God knows where. She would see
guys...yeah....anyway.....along comes this
guy. A guy we both knew. A guy who was
into cards. A gamblin' man. And he said
that he used to herd cattle in Argentina. I
dunno, maybe he did, and he had a bit of
money. More'n I had at that point in time.
But it was funny, the way he gambled. He
was not safe in the friends that he made. So
his money would come and go real fast....

MIKE
I never heard this one before.

BROTHER
So this guy, your Mom fell for. What? She
went cuckoo over this guy. Well, their affair
went on for a year or so and your mom
wanted to marry this guy. She was already
married to our real dad. So he said no. He
didn't love her anyways. But she wanted him
to marry her. And to have a little family.
That's when you were born. As a matter of
fact, you were really the cause of this whole
mess. She wanted to make a little family and
take you and this guy someplace and set
something up.
    (slaps his leg with his hand)
A family thing! Ridiculous, right. A card
man. Had a bunch of money, but could have
just as well lost it on his next hand. Probably
did too. Well you'll see what I'm getting at.

MIKE
That's not how I heard it.

BROTHER
Yeah, I know. You heard it from me and I'm
telling it different this time, see? So this Mom
of yours found herself a fuckin' gun. I

> BROTHER (continued)
> thought she was going to blow me away with it
> one night. She got so into this gun. She
> would flash it to anybody that gave her
> trouble. She would sleep with it. Yeah...
> strange, huh? She would stir fry vegetables
> with the loaded gun. What? I mean......
> What? I used to say, politely, "Mom, don't go
> stirring up dinner with the gun, now, you'll
> blow a hole in the frying pan." What?

Mike begins to cry.

> BROTHER
> And she used to do other things with this gun.
> Sexy things with it. Oh, boy, she was into
> this thing. I just thought it was some sort of
> weird phase that she was going through. And
> so anyway, this guy, who she was cuckoo
> over, brought her to the movies one night. A
> drive-in movie in a stolen car, don't-cha-
> know, what? And the movie was....ah....RIO
> BRAVO or some shit like that. And well, she
> went and shot this guy....don't-cha-know.

> MIKE
> You're making this up as you go along, bro.

> BROTHER
> And they didn't find him until the next show,
> RIO BRAVO playing on the big screen. Spilled
> popcorn soaking up the blood.

Mike begins to really cry now, bawling and coughing.

> SCOTT
> (who has been listening)
> Oh, come on, how corny, man....

> BROTHER
> No. Your mom had to split, and split she did.
> And that guy. That guy was your real father.

                    MIKE (sniffs)
I knew that was coming. You sure do like to
make me cry, bro.

                    BROTHER
And I got this card from her, not too awful
long ago. Maybe a year.

Mike's Brother hands him a postcard with a Holiday Inn
motel on the front of it. Written on the card, Mike's
mom says she is working as a waitress there, in the
"Blue Room" of the Holiday Inn off Interstate 85 outside
Boise, Idaho. He also hands him a *picture* of his mom.

Mike and Scott wore sunglasses as they journeyed
onward to the Blue Room, Scott driving the motorcycle
and Mike riding on the back.

Night time exterior of the Holiday Inn.

Mike and Scott pull up on the motorcycle and park it.

Inside the Holiday Inn.

A hostess is standing in front of a sign that bills
"Shecky Crude" as the featured entertainer of the
evening in the "Blue Room."

Mike is speaking to the hostess. He shows her his
picture of mom.

                    MIKE
          My mother works here. Her name is Dorothy.

                    HOSTESS
          (thinks for a second)
          No. I can't think of anyone by that name.
          Let me get the manager.

The hostess picks up the phone.

Manager's office night.

A MANAGER is sitting behind his desk wearing a shiny
blue suit, he shifts in his swiveling chair, and looks at
the Holiday Inn Postcard that Mike's mother sent to his
father.

                    MANAGER
          Dorothy, Dorothy.....There was a Dorothy
          Biondi used to work here a year ago, but she
          split. Saved up all her money and headed to
          Italy.

                    MIKE
          To Italy?

                    MANAGER
          Yeah. It took her forever to save any cash,
          but she did, and flew away. She was looking
          for her family. I guess she came from Italy.
          But she didn't look Italian.

                    SCOTT
          Was your mom Italian?

                    MIKE
          I don't know.   I guess that she was.

In the lobby of the Holiday Inn at night.

Mike and Scott witness the arrival of the German
Mercedes Benz parts salesman.

                    SCOTT
          There's that guy.

                    MIKE
          Who?

>   SCOTT
> The guy who gave us a ride from Portland.
> What's he doing here?

Scott and Mike walk up to him. HANS turns and a
broad smile crosses his face.

>   HANS
> Mike! Scottie! How good to run into you! My
> dear boys! How have you been?

Inside Hans' hotel bathroom. Night.

Mike lies in a bathtub in sudsy water. There is a
pounding on the bathroom door.

>   MIKE
> I just got in the tub! Wait your turn.

>   HANS
> But Mike! Don't you want anything to eat? We
> are ordering room service. Ya?

>   MIKE
> Ahhh. Room service? Ya! Let me see.
> Two hamburgers, with cheese, onions, lettuce,
> tomato, no pickles. A Coke and french fries.

>   HANS
> O.K. That's hamburger wiz everything, no
> pickles, Coke, french fries.

>   MIKE
> That is correct.

>   HANS
> Thank you.

>   MIKE
> You're welcome.

As Mike and Scott eat their hamburgers, Hans sits across from them next to a small desk light on a double bed in his Holiday Inn room.

> HANS
> How are the hamburgers, boys?

> MIKE
> They're okay, Hans.

> SCOTT
> Good, Hans. I don't think that I've tasted a hamburger as fine as this Holiday Inn hamburger.

> HANS
> I'm glad that you like it.

The boys eat approvingly.

> HANS
> How did you boys get so far? I only left you in Portland a few days ago.

> SCOTT
> We rode on our trusty motorcycle.

> HANS
> And what brings you to the Holiday Inn?

> SCOTT
> Business.

> HANS
> What kind of business?

> SCOTT
> We're selling motorcycles.

Still images of Mike, Scott and Hans having sex in the motel.

Hans rides his newly purchased motorcycle across the plains from Boise to Picabu, Idaho. A local policeman pulls him over doing 95 mph in a 45 mph zone.

At the Boise Airport Scott and Mike stand in a ticket line. The ticket taker stamps their tickets.

> TICKET TAKER
> Do you have any baggage?

Mike and Scott shake their heads no.

I t a l i A

Mike wakes up and finds himself sitting beside the
Trevi fountain in Rome. There are other street kids
surrounding him fishing for coins that tourists have
thrown in the fountain. He doesn't see Scott.

He looks around a bit.

                         SCOTT (o.s.)
           Mikey! Over here!

Mike's VIEW of Scott in a taxi cab.

The TAXI pulls up to a small farmhouse on a hill
outside of Rome. Mike and Scott get out and walk
around the house. A farmer is cutting his crop on the
next hillside.

A DOG walks up to them.

The taxi driver gets out of the car and asks for his
money in Italian. Scott holds out the money that he
has and the driver takes it, counting it out for himself.

Mike walks around a corner of the house and notices the
doors are open as the cab drives off down the drive.

Scott sits down on the stoop in front of a shack and
Mike steps into the house.

MIKE
Mom? .... Hello?

An extremely *Beautiful Italian girl* walks around the
corner where Scott is sitting. He can't see her. And
she leans against the shack and stares at him, then
looks up at Mike, who is walking through the house
trying to find someone.

GIRL
Hello.

Scott looks up at her, a little surprised.

SCOTT
Hi. Is this your house?

The girl is a little shy and leans on the shack.

GIRL
No. This isn't my house, but. It is my
uncle's house.

SCOTT
I'm Scott.

GIRL
I'm Carmella.

SCOTT
And he is Mike. We came from America to
find his mother.

CARMELLA
Oh. An American woman?

SCOTT
Yeah, do you know her?

CARMELLA
Yes, but. It is not true that she lives here.

SCOTT
It isn't true?

>   CARMELLA
>   No. She left a long time ago. Back to
>   America.
>
>   SCOTT
>   Oh, shit.   Was she your friend?
>
>   CARMELLA
>   I wanted to speak English, and she taught it to
>   me.

Mike walks from the house to Scott and Carmella.

>   CARMELLA
>   Hello. My name is Carmella.
>
>   MIKE
>   I'm Mike.
>
>   CARMELLA
>   Hello Mike.
>
>   SCOTT
>   She knows your mom.

Later in the afternoon, Mike is inside of a room in the house, and he is crying. He is talking to Scottie, who is holding him.

>   MIKE
>   I mean, Christ, we come all this fuckin' way
>   and she ain't here either. Where'd she go
>   from here?

Mike walks through the rooms of the Italian country house.

MIKE'S VIEW of a room, and Scott is just closing the door. He winks at Mike as he shuts it.

Inside the room, Carmella and Scott lay down on the bed and kiss.

Scott takes off his clothes and ravishes Carmella, tearing at her dress.

Carmella is naked and the two grab and twist with each other on the white bed.

Still views of the lovemaking.

Mike in the country, watching the farmer in the field.

Mike approaches the house and there is a taxi cab waiting. Carmella is putting a suitcase in the trunk.

Scott helps Carmella in the front seat of the taxi.

                    SCOTT
          Hey, Mike. Let me talk with you for a second.

Scott follows Mike inside the house and into a room.

                    SCOTT
          I'm gonna take some time off.

Scott gives Mike an American Express card.

                    SCOTT
          Don't leave home without it. Ha-ha.
             (Mike doesn't think it's funny)
          I mean, maybe I'll run into you down the
          road.

Mike is shocked but sees what Scott needs to do as he
looks out the window and can see Carmella in the taxi.

                        MIKE
             Yeah, sure. Okay.

                        SCOTT
             Sorry about this, dude.

                        MIKE
             I'll be okay. Don't worry about me.

                        SCOTT
             Sorry, but....

                        MIKE
             No, man, forget it. Hurry up, she's waiting,
             you're gonna lose her.

Mike hides a tear.

                        SCOTT
             All right. You sure you'll be okay?

                        MIKE
             Go on, get out of here.

Outside, a dog watches the taxi leave down a rutted
dirt drive.

                        MIKE'S THOUGHTS:
             Well. So much for the great protector-of-us-
             all. Protector of himself, more like. I couldn't
             believe Scott would leave me here in the
             middle of a foreign country.

Inside, Mike goes into one of his fits, snorting, a little
like a pig, and falls asleep.

P o R t l a n d

*M*ike wakes up in an airline's passenger seat. A
STEWARDESS is leaning over him.

> STEWARDESS
> Wake up. Wake up, we're here.

> MIKE
> Where? Where am I?

> STEWARDESS
> You're in Portland.

Int. BROADWAY CAFE in the day.

Mike sits at the round table in front of the window.

Denise is with a new boy, STUART, and they are making
out. Mary sits and chain smokes cigarettes, there are
three other UNKNOWNS around the table.

> MIKE
> And so, I was back in Portland, enjoying the
> life I used to lead. It was like I was back from
> a vacation. Denise had a boyfriend now....

Ext. street night.

Cars cruise by. Mike is on a street corner. He hops
into a stranger's car.

Int. MOTEL night.

Still views of Mike having sex with a date.

                    MIKE
          ...and I enjoyed the fruits of my labor.

CLOSE VIEW of money exchanging hands.

BROADWAY CAFE day.

Mike is at the table again, smoking a cigarette.

There are three new kids who look very MEAN, and are
hassling another kid, pulling his collar and throwing
him around.

                    MIKE'S THOUGHTS
          And there were new kids who were coming
          around who wanted to take your money. It
          was a dark period for the streets. Normally,
          Scott would keep order in the Broadway Cafe.

A Hot Dog stand. Gary cheerfully prepares Mike a hot
dog.

                    MIKE'S THOUGHTS
          Gary and Ray both got work at stands.
          It was funny...

Int. Deli day.

Ray serves Mike a hot dog.

> MIKE'S THOUGHTS
> ...they both sold hot dogs. Which is what
> they were used to selling on the streets in the
> old days. These guys had really changed, I
> thought.

Mike's FACE, outdoors in the daytime.

He looks out on the cityscape.

The buildings of the city uproot and tumble in the air.

Jakes restaurant night.

Mike wakes up. He is sitting next to Bob and Budd. A
new friend, a colorfully dressed man named BAD
GEORGE, who looks like a street minstrel, talks on the
street in front of a fancy restaurant. Bad George is
obnoxiously yelling in Bob's face.

> BAD GEORGE
> Bob! What tidings I bring you. And such joy.
> Some of that old rot gut that you and I used
> to drink. I have three bottles stashed in the
> bushes out on eighty-second.

> BOB
> What blew you in?

> BAD GEORGE
> Think of the fun we can have, if we could only
> find a ride for a journey to the bushes where
> the hooch is hid.

                         BOB
        If I shared your wine, I might catch this awful
        disease you appear to have. My clothes would
        turn striped, and I would suddenly have bells
        on my toes, like this here...

Bob points to George's bells on his shoes.

                      BAD GEORGE
        Bob, you're one of the greatest living men on
        Three-street.

                         BOB
        That is correct.

                      BAD GEORGE
        Surely you can find us a ride somewhere.

                     MIKE'S THOUGHTS:
        As I listened to Bad George and Bob talk, I
        watched across the street as a long black car
        pulled up alongside one of the fancier
        restaurant/bar establishments of Portland.
        And who got out of that car? It was the old
        protector-of-us-all, himself.......Scottie
        Favor.

Bob notices the group of men getting out of a car in
front of the restaurant. One of them is Scottie , in a
three pieced suit. He is with his Italian girlfriend.

                         BOB
        If it isn't Scottie Favor himself. Blessed are
        they who have been my close friends. Now
        dressed in a three pieced suit and looking
        every bit a gentleman! He has run into his
        inheritance.

                      BAD GEORGE
        Who?

                         BOB
        George, Budd, Mike. We have waited for this
        day to come.

Bob charges in the direction of Scottie and his friends.

Int. Jakes. Night.

Scottie and his associates, who are men much older
than he, perhaps in their thirties, make their way
through the yuppie crowd standing in the bar drinking.
Hellos and how-do-you-do's are directed at Scottie. A
man stops Scott on his way through the crowd.

> MAN
> Scottie! I haven't seen you in a dog's age.
> You're looking well. So grown up. Scottie, I'd
> like you to meet Ed Warren, he's in marketing
> at Nike. Ed, this is Scottie Favor.

> ED
> Oh, Jack Favor's son, hello, pleased to meet
> you.

> SCOTTIE
> How do you do?

Bob is following Scottie through the crowd. Scottie
walks past Hans, who is having a drink with another
man. They recognize each other but neither speak.

Bob, with Bad George in tow, straightens himself up as
the yuppie crowd looks on disapprovingly. Their smelly
clothing betrays them.

> BOB
> Come, George, watch this. You will see the
> attention that I get.

Bob looks at his clothes. A bouncer spots them.

> BOB
> It's true we're drawing attention to ourselves.
> But Scottie will see that I am dying to see
> him, and it won't matter how we're dressed.

Scotty and his friends are sitting around a crowded
table. As they take their seats, Scottie hears Bob
bellowing.

VIEW of Bob being detained by the bouncer.

>   BOB
>   God save you! God save you, my sweet boy.

Scotty turns away from Bob, so his back is to him.

>   BOB
>   Sonny! My true friend!

Silence for a second, the crowd grows quieter.

>   BOB
>   I mean you, Sonny! It's me, Bob!

Without turning toward Bob, Scottie speaks.

>   SCOTT
>   I don't know you, old man.

>   GIRL IN CROWD
>   Who is that bum?

Scottie turns and meets Bob, who kneels next to him.

>   SCOTTIE
>   Please leave me alone.

Bob is thinking that Scottie's attitude is a joke.

>   SCOTTIE
>   Don't think that I'm the same Scottie that I
>   was before. Everyone has noticed that I have
>   turned away from that life, and the people
>   who kept me company.

Bob is shocked.

Outside, Mike can see through the windows of the restaurant, Bob and Scottie talking.

Int. Jakes. night.

> SCOTTIE
> When I was young, and you were my street
> tutor. An instigator for my bad behavior, I
> was trying to change. Now that I have, and
> until I change back.....don't come near me.

Bob feels the rejection like a shock. Stares at Scott for
a second, then he's pulled away by the bouncer.

Ext. Jakes. night.

Mike watches Bob and Budd sit down with him.

> BUDD
> Don't take all this seriously. It's one of his
> jokes.

Nightime overhead view of Bob in his greasy derelict
hotel bed. He is having nightmares, and suddenly he
CRIES OUT!

> BOB
> God, God....God!

Dawn views of the city.

*M*ike awakes atop a downtown building.

*I*nside the Derelict Hotel Day.

Mike enters, and walks through a very quiet, although
crowded MAIN ENTRANCE. There is a body on a slab in
the middle of the room that is covered with a sheet.

> MIKE
>
> Pigeon?

> A BOY
>
> Scottie Favor broke his heart.

> GARY
>
> He's gone now, either to Heaven or to Hell.

> JANE LIGHTWORK
>
> Be sure it isn't to Hell. He tried to be an
> honest sort. I'm the one who heard him cry
> out last night. He said God, God, God... three
> or four times. And when I got there I put my
> hand into the bed and felt his feet. And they
> were cold as stone. And I checked the rest of
> his body. And it too was as cold as stone.

> BUDD (crying)
>
> It sure is quiet.

Mike approaches Budd.

> MIKE
>
> I guess you're gonna miss him the most, Budd.

Mike gives him Scottie's American Express card, as
others carry his body out of the hotel.

> MIKE
>
> Here. Maybe you can give him a good burial.

Budd cries.

Mike exits.

In the country, Mike looks at the road.

He has visions of sagebrush and rock flying into the air
as if picked up by a big wind.

Then he lies asleep by the side of the road.

>   MIKE'S VOICE
> I suppose that a lot of kids like me think that
> they have no home, that home is a place
> where you have a mom and a dad.

Pause.

>   MIKE'S THOUGHTS
> But home can be any place that you want. Or
> wherever you can find.....My home is right
> here on the side of this road, that I been to
> before. I just know I been on this fucking
> road one time before, you know that?

Later, a car drives by Mike's sleeping body by the side
of the road. It turns around and stops next to Mike. A
figure puts Mike in his car and drives off down the
road.

>   MIKE'S THOUGHTS
> Sometimes I had thought that God had not
> smiled on me, and had given me a bum deal.
> And other times, I had thought that God had
> smiled on me. Like now. He was smiling on
> me...for the time being....

Int. Car. Day.

Scott is driving the car. He looks over at Mike sleeping.

Ext. Desert. Day.

The car disappears down the road.

Gus Van Sant Filmography

Gus Van Sant is director on all titles.

1967
Fun With a Bloodroot
2 minutes 30 seconds, 8mm colour

1971
The Happy Organ
20 minutes, 16mm black and white

1972
Little Johnny
40 seconds, 16mm black and white

1973
1/2 of a Telephone Conversation
2 minutes, 16mm black and white

1975
Late Morning Start
28 minutes, 16mm colour

1978
The Discipline of DE
9 minutes, 16mm black and white

1981
Alice in Hollywood
45 minutes, 16mm colour

1982
My Friend
3 minutes, 16mm black and white

1983
Where'd She Go
3 minutes, 16mm colour

1984
Nightmare Typhoon
9 minutes, 16mm black and white

My New Friend
3 minutes, 16mm colour

1985
Ken Death Gets Out of Jail
3 minutes, 16mm black and white

Mala Noche
Production company: Northern Film Co.
Producer: Gus Van Sant
Production associates: Jack Yost, Chris Monlux
Screenplay: Gus Van Sant, based on the story by Walt Curtis
Cinematography: John Campbell, with Eric Alan Edwards
Sound: Pat Baum
Editor: Gus Van Sant
Music: Creighton Lindsay
Cast: Tim Streeter (*Walt*), Doug Cooeyate (*Johnny*), Ray Monge
      (*Roberto Pepper*), Nyla McCarthy (*Betty, Walt's girl*), Sam
      Downey (*hotel clerk*), Bob Pitchlynn (*drunk man*), Eric Pedersen
      (*policeman*), Marty Christiansen (*bar friend*), Bad George
      Connor (*wino*), Don Chambers (*himself*), Walt Curtis (*George*),
      Kenny Presler (*street hustler*), Conde Benavides (*arcade amigo*),
      Cristo Stoyos (*Greek singer*), Matt Cooeyate (*boxcar amigo*),
      Maruya Munoz (*lady with knife*), Arturo Torres (*voice of
      Johnny*)
78 minutes, 16mm black and white, part in colour

1986
Five Ways to Kill Yourself
3 minutes, 16mm black and white

1989
Drugstore Cowboy
Production company: Avenue Entertainment
Executive producer: Cary Brokaw
Producers: Nick Wechsler, Karen Murphy
Production executives: Laurie Parker, Claudia Lewis
Screenplay: Gus Van Sant, Daniel Yost, based on the novel by James
      Fogle

Production design: David Brisbin
Cinematography: Robert Yeoman, with Eric Alan Edwards
Sound: Dane A. Davis
Music: Elliot Goldenthal
Songs: 'For All We Know' by Fred J. Coots, Sam Lewis, performed
   by Abbey Lincoln, Geri Allen (piano); 'Little Things' by and
   performed by Bobby Goldsboro; 'Psychotic Reaction' by Ken
   Ellner, Roy Chaney, Craig Atkinson, John Byrne, John
   Michalski, performed by The Count Five; 'Put a Little Love in
   Your Heart' by Jimmy Holiday, Randy Myers, Jackie
   DeShannon, performed by Jackie DeShannon; 'Piu amore
   romantico per Anna' by Jeff Levi; 'The Israelites' by Desmond
   Dekker, Leslie Kong, performed by Desmond Dekker & the
   Aces; 'I Am' by Roky Erickson, performed by Roky Erickson,
   Jack Johnson; 'Judi in Disguise' by Fred John, Andrew
   Barnard, performed by John Fred and his Playboy Band;
   'Cherry Lips' by Winfield Scott, performed by The Robins;
   television commercial music by and performed by Will Kaplan
Cast: Matt Dillon (*Bob Hughes*), Kelly Lynch (*Dianne Hughes*),
   James Le Gros (*Rick*), Heather Graham (*Nadine*), Beah
   Richards (*drug counsellor*), Grace Zabriskie (*Bob's mother*), Max
   Perlich (*David*), William S. Burroughs (*Tom the Priest*), Eric
   Hull (*druggist*), James Remar (*Gentry*), John Kelly (*cop*), George
   Catalano (*Trousinski*), Janet Baumhover (*neighbour lady*), Ted
   D'Arms (*neighbour man*), Neal Thomas (*Halamer*), Stephen
   Rutledge (*motel manager*), Robert Lee Pitchlynn (*hotel clerk*),
   Roger Hancock (*machinist*), Mike Parker (*crying boy*), Ray
   Monge (*accomplice*), Woody (*panda*)
101 minutes, 35mm colour

1991
My Own Private Idaho
Production Company: New Line Cinema
Producer: Laurie Parker
Executive Producer: Gus Van Sant
Co-Executive Producer: Allan Mindel
Directors of Photography: Eric Alan Edwards, John Campbell
Editor: Curtiss Clayton
Screenplay: Gus Van Sant, additional dialogue by William
   Shakespeare
Costume Designer: Beatrix Aruna Pasztor
Music: Bill Stafford
Cast: River Phoenix (*Mike Waters*), Keanu Reeves (*Scott Favor*),

James Russo (*Richard Waters*), William Reichert (*Bob Pigeon*),
Rodney Harvey (*Gary*), Chiara Caselli (*Carmella*), Michael
Parker (*Digger*), Jessie Thomas (*Denise*), Flea (*Budd*), Grace
Zabriskie (*Alena*), Tom Troupe (*Jack Favor*), Udo Kier (*Hans*),
Sally Curtice (*Jane Lightwork*), Robert Lee Pitchlynn (*Walt*),
Mickey Cottrell (*Daddy Carroll*), Wade Evans (*Wade*)
104 minutes, 35mm colour

Thanksgiving Prayer
2 minutes 30 seconds, 35mm colour

1993
Even Cowgirls Get the Blues
Production Company: New Line Cinema
Producer: Laurie Parker
Executive Producer: Gus Van Sant
Directors of Photography: John Campbell, Eric Alan Edwards
Production Designer: Missy Stewart
Screenplay: Gus Van Sant, based on the novel by Tom Robbins
Costume Designer: Beatrix Aruna Pasztor
Music: k. d. lang and Ben Mink
Cast: Uma Thurman (*Sissy Hankshaw*), Rain Phoenix (*Bonanza
Jellybean*), Lorraine Bracco (*Delores del Ruby*), John Hurt (*The
Countess*), Angie Dickinson (*Miss Adrian*), Noriyuki 'Pat' Morita
(*The Chink*), Keanu Reeves (*Julian*), Sean Young (*Marie Barth*),
Crispin Glover (*Howard Barth*), Ed Begley Jr. (*Rupert*), Carol
Kane (*Carla*), Victoria Williams (*Debbie*), Dee Fowler (*Kym*),
Arlene Wewa (*Big Red*), Judy Robinson (*Gloria*), Heather
Graham (*Heather*), Elizabeth Roth (*Mary*), Heather Hershet
(*Donna*), Roseanne Arnold (*Madame Zoe*), Buck Henry (*Dr.
Dreyfus*), Ken Kesey (*Sissy's daddy*), Grace Zabriskie (*Mrs.
Hankshaw*), Ken Babbs (*Sissy's uncle*), Udo Kier (*film director*)
108 minutes, 35mm colour

MUSIC VIDEOS

1990
'Fame' David Bowie
'Tarbelly and Featherfoot' Victoria Williams

1991
'Seventeen' Tommy Conwell

1992
'Under the Bridge' Red Hot Chili Peppers
'Bang, Bang, Bang' Tracy Chapman
'Runaway' Deee-Lite
'Last Song' Elton John

1993
'San Francisco Days, San Francisco Nights' Chris Isaak